Under Pressure

"What's wrong, Ashley?" Nikki asked me. "You look upset."

"I was just worrying about the movie," I admitted. "Did I tell you my mom showed up this afternoon?"

"She did? That was nice of her," said Chloe.

"It was," I said. "But somehow it makes me even more nervous. It's just one more person judging me."

"That's a funny way to look at it," said Nikki. "I'm sure she came to be supportive."

"And to make sure I don't goof up and embarrass her," I said. "I didn't need Dad telling everyone I'm going to be a star, either. Why couldn't he just have said, 'This is Ashley, my daughter'? Why wasn't that good enough?"

Cover Kids

Ashley's Big Mistake

Suzanne Weyn

Troll Associates

For Diana Gonzalez

LIBRARY OF CONGRESS CATALOGING-IN-PUBLICATION DATA

Weyn, Suzanne.
    Ashley's big mistake / by Suzanne Weyn.
        p.   cm. — (Cover kids)
    Summary: While visiting her father in California, teenage model
Ashley Taylor has an opportunity to try her skill at acting in a
television movie.
    ISBN 0-8167-3231-0 (lib.)   ISBN 0-8167-3232-9 (pbk.)
    [1. Self-esteem—Fiction.   2. Friendship—Fiction.   Teenage
models—Fiction.   4. Acting—Fiction.   5. Family life—Fiction.
6. Fathers and daughters—Fiction.]   I. Series.
PZ7.W539As   1994
[Fic]—dc20   93-43505

A TROLL BOOK, published by Troll Associates.

10 9 8 7 6 5 4 3 2 1

Ashley's Big Mistake

Chapter One

Here is a letter I sent from California to my very best friend, Chloe Chang. Like me, Chloe is a model with the Calico Modeling Agency. We're in the junior division, for models fifteen and younger. Chloe and I are thirteen, and so are our two other friends at the agency, Tracey Morris and Nikki Wilton.

Anyway, this is what I wrote to her while I was visiting my father.

Dear Chloe,

Greetings from sunny California! Here's the great news. I got the part in the movie! Hooray! Can you believe it? I'll be playing Julie, who is a totally cool character. She's this girl from a poor family who comes to a rich, snooty junior high and meets a girl named Andrea. Then Andrea can't decide whether or not she's too cool to hang out with Julie.

The Andrea character is really the star of the TV movie, which is an Afternoon Movie for Teens special. My part is big enough, though, especially considering that this is my very first acting role. Soon Johnny won't be my mom's only famous kid. I'll be right up there with him—no longer just a model but also a star! Ta-da!

Speaking of Johnny, it's great to see him again, although he's busy working on his TV series. But he comes over a lot in the evenings. My dad and he are really close.

Anyhow, everything is great. Dad's new house is totally gorgeous. It has a pool, a tennis court, and a private beach!

Guess what? Larry Morton, the director of the TV movie, asked me if I had any model friends who would be interested in being cast as extra junior high students in the movie. You know, the kids who sit in class and walk down the hall but don't say actual lines.

Wouldn't it be great if you, Tracey, and Nikki could fly out and be in the movie with me? It would be such a blast! I'm sure my dad wouldn't mind if you guys stayed here. His house is *huge!*

I suppose there's not much chance of that happening since all of you are so busy with school and modeling and all.

How are Nikki and Tracey? I sent them each a postcard, but I'm writing you this letter because you are my very, very best friend. I miss you and wish you could be here. See you soon.

Love,
Ashley

I was super shocked when Chloe replied to my letter by Express Mail. When the flat cardboard envelope came, I didn't know what to expect. Here's what she wrote.

Dear Ashley,

Way to go! Congratulations on getting the part. I know how much it means to you.

I have some awesome news of my own, so make sure you're somewhere where they won't mind if you scream and jump around for joy. I was at the agency the other day, and when Ms. Calico asked me how you were, I showed her your letter. (I didn't think you'd mind since it wasn't too personal.) After she read it, she had this very thoughtful look on her face, as if she was getting a great idea. You know the look. It was her *I have a way to make the modeling agency even better* face. Then she said to me, "Don't you and Nikki and Tracey have a winter break from school coming up?" It's amazing how she keeps track of things like that, but I guess she didn't get to have her own modeling agency by not paying attention. So I told her that yes, we did have break soon. Then she disappeared into her office. At the end of the day, she called in Tracey, Nikki, and me and told us that she'd booked an assignment for all of us in Hollywood!

Are you screaming yet? If you are, save some screams because it gets even better. Ms. Calico wants us all to try out to be extras in your movie while we're out there. She says it would be good for the agency if our faces became more familiar to the public. If that offer to stay with you and your dad is for real, our answer is yes. This is so exciting.

Love,
Chloe

Chloe was right. I did start to scream and jump around.

As soon as Dad got home from the set—he's a TV director—I asked if my friends could stay with us. "Sure, no problem," he said, as he sat on a lounge chair near the pool and thumbed through papers in a cream-colored folder.

"Really?" I asked happily.

"Uh-huh," he said, still searching for the paper he wanted. He ran a tan hand through his longish blond hair and leaned forward on the chair. In his Hawaiian print shirt and baggy white pants, he looked young and stylish. I've heard people say my dad is very handsome, and I suppose he is.

"Can I have a red sports car?" I asked. I was testing to find out if he was really listening to me.

"Sure, no problem," he said, pulling a paper from the folder.

"And I think I should get one hundred thousand dollars a week as an allowance," I went on.

That got his attention. He looked up at me as if he was seeing me for the first time. "I'm sorry, honey. What did you say?"

I sighed, and my hands went to my hips. "I want my friends to stay here when they come to California! Did you hear that part?"

From his expression, I could tell he hadn't. "Sure," he said. "I mean, I didn't hear you, but it's fine. This place is as big as a hotel. Why not?"

"Thanks, Dad!" I cried.

"Sorry I was distracted," Dad said. "The writers added a new character to the TV movie I'm working on. I have to find an actress by tomorrow."

"Hollywood is full of actresses," I commented. "How hard could that be?"

"It's hard because I'm looking for a particular type. I'm known for finding good people. I have to keep up my reputation. What people say about you is very important in this business."

"Is it like modeling?" I asked. "If people start saying you're hard to work with or you're unprepared, then you don't work as much."

"Yes, it's like that, but much more intense. Show business is more competitive than modeling. You have to be on top of things every second," he replied.

"Gee, I thought modeling was pretty competitive," I said.

"Wait—you'll find out. Show business is much harder," he said. "Anyway, in a few days I'll have more time to spend with you. By then things will have settled down on this project."

"That's okay," I said. "I understand." I knew he'd let my friends stay. My dad is a pretty easygoing guy, and he gives me almost anything I ask for. Too bad I see him only a few months each year.

Of course, I couldn't wait to tell Chloe, Nikki, and Tracey to come to California as soon as they could. Even overnight mail seemed too slow, so I got permission to make a long-distance call.

Just as I placed my hand on the receiver, the phone rang. "Hello?" I said.

"Ashley, dear," came the familiar voice on the other end. It was Kate Calico, who is just about the most beautiful, sophisticated woman on earth. She used to be a model herself, before founding the Calico agency.

"Hi, Kate," I said. I call her by her first name since I know her so well. I've been modeling with her agency nearly all my life. "Chloe wrote me about what's going on. My dad says it's fine if she, Tracey, and Nikki stay with us. I can't wait to see them."

"Thank you, Ashley, but there are a few details still to be ironed out. Is your father at home?"

"Sure. I'll get him."

I ran with the cordless phone to Dad's office. He was watching a video of the scenes of his movie that had been filmed that day. "Kate needs to talk to you," I said, handing him the phone.

Using the remote control, he snapped off the TV and took the phone. "Kate," he said in his friendly way, "what's happening?"

I stood and watched as Dad talked to her. Mostly he just kept nodding and saying, "Sure, no problem." Once in a while, he laughed loudly at something Kate said. As they talked, he turned on the VCR again and watched it with the sound off. "I'll have Phyllis, my secretary, call their parents if you like," he offered. Then he nodded some more. "Okay, very good. We'll stay in touch."

Dad clicked off the phone and smiled at me. His blue eyes were all twinkly. "It looks like your girlfriends are on their way here, kitten."

"Yes!" I cried, jumping up and punching the air.

"It's not a totally sure thing," he warned. "I have to talk to their parents and assure them that you girls will be properly looked after."

"Mr. and Mrs. Chang know you," I said, "so that will be okay. They'll let Chloe come. Tracey's mother isn't very strict, so I think she'll let Tracey come, too. The only problem might be Nikki's parents. They're sort of old-fashioned types. Be like a real dad when you talk to them."

"I *am* a real dad, aren't I?" my father said, putting his hand to his heart and pretending to be offended.

"Yeah, of course you're a real dad, but you know what I mean," I said. "Act like a regular dad, not a Hollywood TV director dad. Nikki's parents are pretty strict. They think Nikki is still a baby."

Dad tucked his chin in and stuck out his stomach to make himself look fat. "Do you mean I should pretend I'm an ogre dad and say, 'I'll have Nikki in bed by eight, and she'll have absolutely no fun, and I'll watch her like a hawk'?" he said in a deep, funny voice.

I laughed. My dad can always make me laugh. "Yes, that would be about right," I agreed. "That would convince them to let her come."

"Okay, then that's exactly what I'll do," he said. "Come on, let's go out to the pool and do some serious laps before dinner."

We walked outside to the big in-ground pool. My dad went into the narrow cabana on the deck at the far end of the pool and came out in his striped swimming trunks.

I was already wearing my white one-piece suit with gold trim. I felt as if I'd been in a bathing suit ever since I arrived in Los Angeles. All that was about to change, because in two days I would report to the movie set for the first read-through of the script.

My half brother, Johnny, had set the whole thing up. Actually his agent had arranged the audition. But I had competed against other actresses my age, and I'd gotten the part fair and square.

Gracefully my dad dived into the deep end of the pool. I dived in after him. He swam laps every evening, and during my visit I'd joined him. It was great to be doing stuff with him. Father-and-daughter stuff.

Back home, my mother is always so busy. She pays attention to me, but she's a very businesslike person. She makes time to sit and talk to me at night. I feel like I have to fill her in on what I'm doing, how I'm feeling, and what's coming up for me—all in the hour she sets aside for me. Though it's great that she saves the hour, sometimes I'd just like to let things flow a little more naturally. But between her career as a TV personality and my career as a model, not to mention doing schoolwork, there's not a whole lot of time.

Still, Mom does pretty well when you consider how busy her schedule is. You see, my mom is the TV talk show host Taylor Andrews, and she has the number-one-rated morning talk show. She gets up at four every morning so she can be on the air by seven. When the show ends at nine, she starts working on the next day's program until about six at night. She's usually home by six-thirty, but she has to go to bed early in order to be at work bright and early the next morning.

I live with Mom most of the year. But I go to California to visit my father whenever I can. I've been doing that from the time I was seven, which was when they were divorced.

For a while Johnny lived with Mom and me. He's my half brother from Mom's first marriage, but because he's lived with me since I was born, I think of him as just my plain old brother.

When Mom remarried, Johnny didn't like her new husband, so he moved to California to try to be a star. Pretty soon he was on a very popular TV show called "One Ashford Avenue," about all these cool young telephone repair guys who share a house. He's what is considered a teen heartthrob. I suppose he is pretty handsome with his long brown hair and high cheekbones. But to me, he's just Johnny, my brother.

As I was swimming, I suddenly heard a splash. Someone else had dived into the pool and was now gliding beneath the aqua water like a shark. Dad hadn't even noticed. He just kept swimming in his determined way. I stopped at the deep end of the pool and hung on to the side, waiting to see who it was.

"Johnny!" I cried as his head popped up out of the water.

He flicked back his long hair, spraying me with water. "Hey, Ashes," he greeted me. "How's it going?"

"Great," I said. "How's the show?"

"Oh, things are nuts on the set. I've been working from five in the morning until nine at night," he said, treading water.

"Oh, you poor dear," I teased. "My heart is just breaking for you. It's so hard to be a star."

Johnny splashed me and I splashed back. Then he poked my shoulder. "Race you."

The next second we were charging across the pool making tidal waves. Johnny is twenty and a lot bigger than I am. But I'm a fast swimmer. I'd never beaten him before; maybe this time I could.

Johnny slapped the side of the pool just seconds before I did. "Ha!" he laughed. "You're getting fast, Ashes."

"Don't call me that," I said. "I hate it."

"Sorry, Ashley dear," he teased. He's called me Ashes since I was little, so I knew he wasn't going to stop. It was such an ugly nickname, though.

"Hey, Johnny!" my father called. He'd stopped at the shallow end of the pool. Johnny stroked through the water toward him. They slapped each other's hands. "What's happening on the set?" Dad inquired.

"Don't ask," said Johnny. "Angela is doing another star

trip, acting like she's the only actress on the show. She's holding the producers up for more money. Nobody knows if she's going to be replaced or not. It's a mess. How's your project?"

Dad complained about the writers on his movie. He didn't like the work they were doing. He wanted rewrites, but then they rewrote too much and he had to add characters. "They don't seem to understand that I have a budget and a schedule to stick to," he groaned.

A shiver ran through me. I wanted to keep moving. "Hey, you two," I scolded. "This is swim time, not work time."

"You're right, kitten," Dad agreed. "The victory goes to the swift and the strong. Or something like that. Swim on!"

Dad, Johnny, and I swam fifteen laps before I stopped at one end of the pool to catch my breath. I heard the sound of a phone ringing. Maybe it was Chloe. Quickly I climbed out of the pool and hurried, soaking wet, into the house.

Mary, the housekeeper, already had the cordless phone. "It's for you," she said, handing me the phone. "Now, shoo, out of here. You're dripping water all over the place."

With the phone in my hand, I went back outside. "Hi," I said as I sat on a lounge chair by the pool.

"It's me," said Chloe. "We're still at the agency. Kate just gave each of us our tickets."

"California, here we come," I heard Nikki shout into the phone.

"All three of you can come?" I asked.

"Nikki's parents want to talk to your dad, but Kate already talked to them, and you know how persuasive she can be," said Chloe.

"Hi, star!" Tracey's voice came from the background.

"When will you get here?" I asked.

"Tomorrow," Chloe replied.

"Tomorrow!" I shrieked. "Cool!"

After getting a pen and some paper, I wrote down all their flight information and then said good-bye. To tell the truth, California had been a little boring so far. But that was all about to change. Dad was going to have more time to spend with me. Johnny was here. My best friends were about to show up. And I was starting work on my very first movie. What could be better? I was about to have the best time of my life!

Chapter Two

---◆---

The next morning, Johnny was over bright and early. He arrived in time to have breakfast with us by the pool. "These look good," he said, pulling up a chair and grabbing a crumb cake from the tray Mary had set out. "Hey, Ashes, your hair is already getting even blonder from the sun."

"Don't call me Ashes!" I told him for the billionth time. "Do you really think it's blonder?" That would be great. I'd look like a real California girl.

Dad and Johnny started talking about some head cameraman they didn't like. "His POV is totally weird," Johnny complained.

"What's POV?" I asked.

"It's short for point of view," Dad told me.

"Oh," I said.

"I had trouble with him, too," Dad said to Johnny. "He tries to do a Hitchcock thing, but it doesn't work."

"Hitchcock thing?" I questioned.

"He thinks he can make his shots look like the ones in Alfred Hitchcock movies," Johnny explained quickly.

I tried to recall an Alfred Hitchcock movie, but I couldn't think of any. I don't pay that much attention to who directs movies. "What's he done lately?" I asked.

"Nothing," Dad said with a smile. "He's dead."

"Oh, too bad," I said.

Johnny went on complaining about this cameraman. "His long shots are from a million miles away, and then he uses the zoom like a madman. The gaffer can't keep up with what he's doing. And the best boy is totally in the dark. It's a disaster."

What were they talking about? I had a million questions, but I didn't want to interrupt again. I felt like I'd already asked enough questions. So instead, I just sat there and felt completely left out. I didn't like the way Johnny was hogging my father and talking a strange language I couldn't understand.

"We'd better get going," I said to Dad after another ten minutes of TV talk. "We have to pick up my friends."

Dad checked his gold watch and grimaced. "Sorry, kitten, no can do."

"What?" I yelped.

22

"I have to be at the studio. Tell you what, though. I'll drive my Porsche, and Cam will take you to the airport." Cam is Dad's chauffeur.

"Okay, I guess," I pouted.

"Your friends will love it," Dad said, getting up. "Being picked up in a chauffeur-driven car is a lot more impressive than meeting someone's boring old dad."

"You're not exactly boring or old," I told him. He and Johnny looked more like brothers than father and stepson.

"Hey, you just made my day." Dad laughed.

"I'd come with you, but you know how it is," said Johnny apologetically. "Fans and all."

"Sure," I said, sulking.

"Wait until your turn comes," Johnny said. "You'll see what a pain it is."

My turn. That sounded good. I didn't think I'd ever consider adoring fans to be a pain.

Dad called Cam on the intercom and asked him to take me to the airport. Cam drove along the streets lined with palm trees without talking. We turned onto the highway and soon got to the airport.

Cam waited in the car while I went inside. The Los Angeles airport wasn't nearly as big and confusing as some airports I'd been in. When my friends' flight landed, I hurried to meet it.

The first one I spotted was Nikki. She's hard to miss because she's tall, beautiful, and has wonderful reddish hair. She's totally the all-American girl.

Next I saw Tracey. She's pretty hard to miss, too. She's as tall as Nikki, with very dark brown hair cut at a blunt angle to her chin. She has the most amazing aqua blue eyes, but she usually conceals them by wearing dark sunglasses. She's really smart and acts super cool and a little tough. I suspect that she's not nearly as tough as she tries to pretend, although her act can be pretty convincing.

Last, but absolutely not least, I saw my best bud, Chloe. Chloe is *not* as easy to spot since she's on the small side. In fact, Chloe worries that she won't grow tall enough to be an adult model. The fashion industry likes models to be tall.

"Hey, you guys!" I called, waving my arm wildly.

"Ashley!" they all cried at once as they ran toward me. The next thing I knew, I was being wrapped in hugs. It was great. In a way, I think of them as sisters more than friends. I felt like I was being reunited with my modeling family.

We quickly got their baggage and dragged it out to Cam, who was waiting at the curb. Then we piled into the car. The backseat was big enough for all four of us.

"Six hours ago we were in snow," Nikki said, as we drove along and the warm breeze blew back her hair. "It's gorgeous here. Look at those palm trees. This is great!"

"I hope you brought your bathing suits," I said.

"Of course we did," said Chloe. "Besides, we'll be

modeling bathing suits. The shoot Kate set up is for California Juniors, which sells bathing suits and sportswear for teens. She said to tell you that they need a blond girl, so she told them you'd take that spot."

"I hope I'll have time with the movie and all," I said.

"It's just a two-day shoot," said Chloe.

"Are we definitely going to be in the movie?" Tracey asked.

"Yep," I said. "Dad called Larry, the director, last night and told him you'd be flying out."

"Unbelievable," said Nikki, hugging herself with excitement. She and Tracey have only been modeling for a few months. They were discovered in a talent search that the Calico agency conducted. Both their lives have changed a lot since then. One minute they were just leading regular junior high kinds of lives, and the next minute they were flying to different places and having their pictures taken—super busy all the time. It's been a big adjustment for them, but they're both handling it pretty well.

When we got to Dad's sprawling split-level house, Cam parked in the three-car garage. We took the inside stairs up to Dad's all-white living room. "How beautiful," Nikki said.

"Would you consider this a mansion?" asked Tracey, who lives with her mother in a small apartment.

"No," I told her. "If you really want to see some awesome mansions, we can take a trip into Beverly Hills someday. Wait until you see some of the stars' homes there."

I showed them to their rooms down a hall off the living room. Nikki and Tracey would be sharing a room, and Chloe would be using the extra twin bed in my room. I was admiring the coolest pair of black-and-white-striped leggings, which Chloe was unpacking, when Mary called, "Phone for you, Ashley!"

I ran to get it, wondering who it could be. The line was filled with static as I picked up the receiver. "Hello? Hello?" I shouted into the phone.

"Ashley, it's Mom," my mother shouted. That explained the static. She was in Brazil filming a series on the rain forests for her talk show.

"Hi, Mom," I shouted. "How's it going?"

"Great. I'm calling to congratulate you on your new role. I called Johnny and he told me all about it. I'm so happy for you, honey."

"Thanks, Mom." Then the line began fuzzing up really badly. When the static died down, I was just able to hear my mother say she had to go.

"Bye, Mom," I said as static blared in my ear one last time. It was nice of her to call, despite the phone lines being messed up. I liked knowing she was thinking of me even while she was in a rain forest.

That afternoon after lunch, I showed my friends the beach that is part of Dad's property. It's just a small patch of sand surrounded by rocks and bushes, and you have to go down an overgrown path to get there, but once you arrive, there's something magic about the spot. Maybe it's the way the surf crashes up against the shore, or the way the ocean seems to stretch out forever in front of you. Or maybe it's simply that it's a private spot hidden away from the world.

"Your own beach!" cried Tracey as she stepped off the scrubby path onto the sand. "What more could a person want?"

"This is like the West Coast version of the Red Room." Chloe laughed, dropping her black-and-white canvas beach bag onto the sand. The Red Room is our secret meeting place at the Calico agency. It's really a darkroom for photo developing that was used by Kate's photographer husband. It has red lights in it because her husband says he creates best in red light. It turns out that he never uses the room anymore—but we do. It's our own sort of clubhouse within the agency.

"Only, this beach has a much better view than the Red Room," Nikki said. That was putting it mildly, since the Red Room has no windows at all.

We spent the rest of the afternoon either in the water or sitting on our beach blankets and talking. "It's so great to do nothing at all," Tracey said, stretching out lazily.

"Enjoy it now, because tomorrow we're going to the studio," I told her.

"We have a shoot the day after tomorrow," said Chloe, rubbing sunblock on her arms. "Will that be a problem?"

"I don't think so," I said. "At least it won't be for you. Tomorrow he just wants to meet the entire cast and crew. Then I think you'll be able to go. The main cast will be reading through the script. I'm not sure what's going on the day after tomorrow. I think you'll be free, but I'm not sure about me."

"I am completely terrified and I don't even have a line," Nikki admitted. "How are you feeling, Ashley?"

"Scared and excited at the same time," I replied. "This is my chance to really *be* somebody."

"But you're already somebody," Nikki said. "You're one of the top junior models at the agency. No one works as much as you do. Your face is on signs and magazines and on TV. If you're not somebody, who is?"

I thought about that a moment. "Johnny is somebody. My mother is definitely somebody. Dad isn't famous, but he's an important guy out here. People who know show business know him."

"What does that make me, nobody?" Tracey asked brusquely.

"No," I said. "Of course you're somebody to yourself and to the people who love you. But in my family, you have to be *somebody* in order to be somebody."

"Oh, that makes a whole lot of sense," Tracey said snidely. "Thanks for explaining it."

I sighed in exasperation. "It's hard to explain."

"I know what she means," Chloe said, coming to my rescue. "Everybody is so famous in her family that it's hard to feel important unless you're famous, too."

"You're one of the busiest models around," Nikki said.

"That's not good enough," I insisted. "I want to be a really, really big star. A megastar. I want to be the most famous person in my whole family."

"Will that make you the best person in your whole family?" Tracey asked skeptically. "Is that what you think?"

"I won't be the least important anymore," I replied.

Unexpectedly a lump formed in my throat, and a mist of tears sprang to my eyes. I shook my head and straightened my shoulders. Starting tomorrow, all that was definitely going to change.

Chapter Three

———◆———

The next morning I got up and dressed in a green-and-yellow-flowered sundress. I tied back my hair with a gold mesh ribbon and slipped on a pair of gold flats. I'd been planning this outfit for days. It was my first-day-on-the-set outfit, casual yet oozing star quality. I didn't want to seem like I was trying too hard, but I was determined to make a good impression.

As I was adjusting the mesh bow for the eight zillionth time, Chloe came back from the shower. She ruffled her short black hair with the towel draped around her neck and then slipped into a black-and-white-checked short-sleeved top and black bike shorts. "I'm almost ready," she said as she pulled on her yellow high-tops. That's Chloe's signature look, black and white with a bold dash of color somewhere in the outfit.

Just then Tracey and Nikki appeared at my bedroom door. Nikki looked terrific as always in a simple pair of baggy cotton pants and a melon-colored T-shirt.

Tracey looked like, well . . . like Tracey. Which means, she looked a little offbeat. She had on longish cutoffs, yellow socks and blue high-tops, a sleeveless orange T-shirt, and a denim vest. Of course she wore her dark sunglasses, too.

Tracey and I would never have the same sense of style, but I admired her individuality. Well, I admired it up to a certain point, anyway. "Please don't wear those glasses onto the set, okay?" I asked her.

"Why not?" she replied, offended.

"Because you're my friend and you look like a nut with them on," I said.

"If I can't wear these glasses in California, then where will I ever be able to wear them?" Tracey asked.

"Nowhere, and that would be good," I said.

"I have to wear these glasses," Tracey insisted. "They tell people that I don't want to express my personality to the world."

"Tracey, you *must* be a genius—an insane genius," I said. "I don't want to be embarrassed."

"Me? Embarrass you?" Tracey said in surprise. "If that's how you feel, forget it."

"She doesn't feel that way," Nikki quickly put in.

"No, I don't," I admitted honestly. "I'm sorry, Tracey.

I'm just nervous, I guess. You look fine." I felt really terrible about what I'd said to Tracey. Up until that minute, I hadn't realized how truly nervous I was.

"Well, okay," Tracey said, still sulking.

"I didn't mean it," I assured her.

Luckily the bad feelings blew over, and we were all in a good mood by the time Cam dropped us off at the studio.

We walked inside and were instantly hit with a blast of air-conditioning. Across the mostly empty room, I spotted Larry Morton, the director. He was a tall man with black hair, a black beard, and wire-rimmed glasses. "Come on," I said to my friends. "I'll introduce you to the director."

We passed a group of people working on camera equipment. I wondered if any of them would want to do a Hitchcock thing. A man and a woman dragged heavy cables across the floor. Above us, bright lights dangled from the ceiling. "Let me see a pink gel on light thirteen," a man shouted. Instantly the light switched from white to pink.

As we crossed the room, I noticed some other actors starting to arrive, guys and girls about my age. "Hi, Larry," I said when we got to him.

Larry looked at me, and for a second I had the awful feeling he didn't know who I was. But then the blank look left his face. "Hi," he said.

"These are my friends Nicole Wilton, Tracey Morris, and Chloe Chang. They're models and they're here to be extras," I told him.

"Terrific," said Larry. "Chloe, I know I've seen your face in ads. You other girls are new models, is that right?"

"Nikki is already the Cotton Kids girl," I told him. "And Tracey is the only model they use for Dingaling cupcakes."

"Super," said Larry. "I'm glad you girls will be with us. I'll tell the camera crew to feature you. Celeb faces give the film a high-budget feel."

"We're celeb faces!" Nikki squealed excitedly. "What do we do first?"

"Nothing," said Larry.

"What?" Tracey said, surprised.

"Nothing today," Larry explained. "We don't need non-speaking actors today. I just wanted to meet everyone. You girls are welcome to stay for the read-through, but we won't really need you until tomorrow when we start blocking scenes."

"Blocking scenes?" I questioned.

"Yes. That means figuring out where everyone stands and moves," said Larry. From the way his eyebrow arched, I could see he was surprised that I didn't know the term. "You have done this before, haven't you?" he asked.

"Not exactly," I admitted.

Larry took a deep breath. He looked sort of annoyed.

"I know a lot from my family, though," I said quickly.

"And modeling has made me very good at holding positions."

"It's okay," he said. "I assumed you'd have more experience, but I'm sure you'll be fine. You seem like a smart kid."

I noticed that Larry kept looking at Chloe. "I wish I'd seen you earlier," he said to her. "You'd be perfect for this movie. You have a great face, so much expression."

"Thanks," said Chloe with a smile.

A hot flame of jealousy flared up in me. I hoped he didn't mean she'd be better for *my* part. I pushed that idea out of my head. I didn't want to be jealous of Chloe. After all, she's my best friend.

A tall girl with red hair in a tight spiral perm came up to us. She placed her hand on Larry's arm. "Larry, when are we beginning? I'm on a tight schedule. I have to finish filming 'Kids Are Cool' at two."

I recognized the girl because I'd seen her on TV before, although I didn't know her name. "This is Delia Carrol," Larry said, introducing her. "She'll be playing the starring role of Andrea." Then he looked at me apologetically. "I'm sorry, but I've forgotten your name. Don't get me wrong— I know who you are. You're Taylor Andrews' kid, and John Renee's sister, and Ted Hoffritz's kid, but your name just escapes me at the moment. Sorry."

"Ashley," I told him, trying not to let him see how mortified I was.

"Ashley Hoffritz?" Larry asked.

"No, Ashley Taylor."

"Is that your stage name?" Delia asked.

"It's my modeling name, actually. Legally my name is still Ashley Hoffritz."

"Keep it as Ashley Taylor. It sounds better," Larry advised, nodding.

"I'll say," Delia agreed. I didn't like the snide way she said that. In fact, although I tried not to judge Delia right away, she had a very unpleasant expression on her face. Her thin lips had an ever-so-slight sneer that made her look as if she was amused by some secret joke. I'm a good judge of people, and I didn't like Delia Carrol much.

Tracey lifted her sunglasses and smiled at me. "I like Ashley Hoffritz better," she teased.

"You would," I teased back.

"It's more like a real person's name," Tracey insisted.

Larry looked around at the actors and extras who'd come in and then clapped his hands sharply. "All right! Cast of *A Bridge of Love* pull up some folding chairs," he called to everyone. "We're going to read through. Extras, sign in with my assistant, Dwight, over there, and you may leave. Be back on Wednesday, though, same time."

While I pulled over a folding chair, Nikki, Tracey, and Chloe signed in with Dwight, a skinny guy with long brown hair tied back in a ponytail. "We're going to walk around and look for stars," Chloe told me when they were done. "We'll be back around lunchtime."

"Okay, good luck," I said.

"Same to you," said Nikki.

When the chairs were all drawn together in a circle, a production assistant handed each of the cast members a fat blue book. It was the TV movie script.

I opened the book. On the third page, I found a list of characters and a quick description of them. Mine read, *Julie . . . a poor but proud girl. Doesn't fit in with middle-class kids at school. Would like friends but fears rejection.*

I read down the list and saw that my character had an older brother. Looking around, I tried to figure out which actor they'd picked for that part. Then my eyes lit on a blond boy with large blue eyes. He looked more like my brother than Johnny did. It had to be him.

Before we began reading, we had to introduce ourselves, say what part we played, and tell a little about ourselves. Sure enough, the boy I'd picked out was my brother. "I'm Jack Jameson," he said. "I play Matt, Julie's brother. I live here in Hollywood. This is my second TV movie role. My first one was in *Locker Madness.* I got that part because a talent scout named Suzie Mendolsohn saw me walking down the hall in school and thought I had the right look for the part."

Suzie Mendolsohn was the woman I'd auditioned for. She's also the casting director for Johnny's show, "One Ashford Avenue."

When my turn came, I smiled at everyone. "My name is Ashley Taylor." I saw Delia smirk when I said that. "I'm a model with the Calico Modeling Agency. This is my first acting role. And . . . um . . . that's all."

Delia leaned toward the girl sitting next to her. "Another airhead model who thinks she can act," she whispered just loudly enough for everyone to hear.

Larry shot her a warning glance, but it didn't really help my embarrassment. What did help, though, was that Jack looked at me and rolled his eyes in Delia's direction. That made me smile.

After the introductions were over—which took a while because we had to listen to all of Delia's TV and movie credits starting from when she was three—we began reading the script. The first time, we went through the script without stopping. It was a breeze. But then Larry had us read through a second time. This time he stopped everyone continually. He stopped if an actor pronounced a word wrong, or if the actors were reading too fast or too slow. He stopped to discuss the feelings behind the words. We even stopped to discuss if characters might actually be thinking something other than what they were saying. It started to become pretty complicated.

I got hung up on the word *predilection* in one of my lines. Larry explained that it means to show a preference for something. No matter how hard I tried, I just couldn't seem to pronounce it correctly. It was as if my tongue had suddenly grown too fat and wouldn't make the right sounds. "Do you think a kid would really use this word?" I asked, after an eternity of trying to say it.

"A smart kid would," said Delia snidely.

Larry ignored her. "Maybe not. I'll talk to the writers about it. Let's keep going."

How embarrassing not to be able to speak properly. At the very least, I'd thought I was good at talking! Things were not going the way I'd hoped.

When the second read-through was done, my head was spinning. "Before we break for lunch," Larry said, "let's go through a little tai chi to unwind."

I knew that tai chi was a series of graceful movements, but I had no idea how to do it. All the other kids seemed to know what was going on, though. They stood and began doing movements that looked like a cross between ballet and karate. I tried to join in, but I couldn't really keep up.

"All right, everyone," said Larry. "You have an hour for lunch, and then I'll see you back here for walk-throughs."

Walk-throughs! I'd thought I was done for the day. "What's a walk-through?" I asked Jack, who was standing nearby.

"That's when you stand and go through the parts with the script in your hand. It's the first stage of blocking."

"Blocking? Oh, yeah, I remember, blocking. That's where everyone is moving, right?"

"Right," said Jack.

"Thanks," I said, feeling pretty dismal. "Where did you learn that tai chi stuff?"

"My movement teacher showed me," Jack said.

There was turning out to be a lot more to acting than I had thought. A lot more!

When it came to modeling, I was number one. I was determined to be number one at this, too.

Chapter Four

—◆—

Early the next morning, Cam drove my friends and me to the Azure Shores Hotel and Resort. That was the location for the California Juniors photo shoot. Lucky for me, I didn't have to be at the studio until that afternoon. Larry wanted to go through some scenes with the star, Delia Carrol.

"Dad would have driven us," I told my friends, "but he had another early call on the set. This movie he's working on is turning out to have a billion problems."

"That's too bad," said Nikki. "He probably wishes he could spend more time with you."

"Yeah, I know," I said. But the truth was, I wasn't so sure. When I was younger, he used to bring me along with him and sort of stick me in a corner while he worked. It made me feel like we were spending time together. This time, though, I was old enough to be left alone. And that was how I was starting to feel—alone.

As soon as Cam dropped us off at the hotel, we were met by Gloria, the clothing company representative. She gave us the clothes we were to model and then directed us to a room where we could change.

We walked into the elegant beachfront hotel room and threw our clothing on the bed. I was glad to be spending this time with my friends. They had been super supportive when I told them about the hard time I'd had the day before. They all agreed that Delia Carrol sounded like a horror show and encouraged me to hang in there.

"Did you ask Johnny about coaching your dialogue?" Chloe called from the bathroom, where she was pulling on a striped one-piece bathing suit.

"He said he could get his speech coach to help me. He's the same guy Mom went to before I was born," I told them. My mother spoke so beautifully, in a smooth, flowing voice, that I couldn't imagine her ever speaking any differently. But according to my father, she'd had a very slight lisp and her voice was too whispery. The voice coach had helped her fix that. "Johnny just started going to him. I didn't know that. I knew he was taking movement classes and fencing lessons. I thought the fencing was just for fun. It turns out that taking fencing is like another movement class. Lots of actors do it."

Tracey threw herself on one of the beds with a bounce. She was already dressed in a cute blue romper. "You sound okay to me. You move all right, too. I mean, what's the big deal? You talk and you walk."

"I thought so, too," I admitted as I fiddled with the back hook of my two-piece suit. "But you have to do things a certain way in show business. You have to speak clearly and move gracefully. My dad told me that the normal way people talk often sounds bad in a movie or TV show. Like you might talk too loud or too fast. Or your voice might be flat and nasal. He says that's all right in regular life, but when people are sitting and listening to you, every little speech defect is magnified and can become really annoying."

"Wow," said Tracey, who was now brushing her hair. "I don't think you have an annoying voice, though."

"Thanks," I replied. "But maybe I do. Johnny also offered to listen to me read my part and give me some pointers. Even though he's not a real coach, I'm sure he can help."

"That's so nice of him," said Chloe, coming out of the bathroom. Chloe thinks Johnny is gorgeous. She's not alone, of course. Johnny just thinks of her as a little kid, however, and it drives her crazy.

When we were ready, we went out onto the beach. It was only eight-thirty in the morning, and the beach was still pretty empty. We met Stefan, a tall, blond photographer who would be taking our pictures for California Juniors. "Beautiful!" he said when he saw us. "Four different versions of the American girl."

I wasn't exactly sure what that meant, but after the terrible day I'd had yesterday, I was glad to hear any kind of praise.

We followed Stefan down the beach and began posing for him. Gloria was there, handing us shorts and beach cover-ups to model. It felt really good to be doing something I did well.

"Take twenty minutes to change and relax," said Stefan at last. "I have to make a few phone calls." We ran to the hotel room and changed into different outfits.

Chloe and I were finished first, so we went back down to the beach with time to spare. "Hey, look," said Chloe, pointing down the shoreline.

I peered along the shore and saw that a crowd of people had gathered. Two vans were also parked on the beach. "Let's see what's going on," I suggested.

We walked over. Right away I recognized the teen actors who were standing in the middle of the crowd, acting out a scene. They were on "Freshman Bell," which was a big hit on one of the cable networks. The show was about these high school freshmen. Although it had a serious side, the show was also hysterically funny.

"Cut!" the director yelled. He strode into the group of actors, looking pretty concerned about something. "This scene is too serious," he said. "Something funny should happen. But what?"

"I know," one of the girls in the show said. "What if, after all the trouble my character goes to to make the best sand castle on the beach, someone walks by and trips over it?" She pointed to a very large, beautiful sand castle several feet away.

A boy with a small, black Scottie on a leash spoke up next. "Yeah, and Petey here goes over and licks the face of the person who falls."

The director rubbed his chin. "That just might work," he said thoughtfully. He looked up and surveyed the crowd. "I don't have time to wait for another actor to audition. I need someone right now. And I'll need someone with a really expressive face because I want the camera to zoom in tight when Petey approaches."

This was a great chance for me. I could add an appearance on "Freshman Bell" to my list of acting credits. I stood tall and smiled my most dazzling model's smile. It seemed to work, too. The director immediately began looking at me.

I stood even taller and smiled even brighter.

He walked right over and said, "You—do you have any acting experience?"

Only he wasn't talking to me. He was talking to Chloe.

"Me?" She giggled. "No, but I'm a model."

"Good enough," he said. "I'm sure you can fall down, can't you?"

"Sure," Chloe replied gamely. He put his arm around Chloe's shoulders and drew her over to the sand castle, talking to her in a low voice I could no longer hear.

Boy, did I feel dumb. I was so sure he was about to pick me. I was glad for Chloe, of course, but the real truth is that I was used to being picked for things before Chloe. I'm the more popular model, probably because I have a more all-American blond kind of look. It's a look a lot of clients want. So not getting this part was a bit of a surprise.

I could handle it, though. After all, Chloe is my best friend.

Chloe did great, too. Better than great. When Chloe is in the mood, she can be pretty funny. The director helped her practice a few falls in the sand. Then the cameras started rolling, and the comedic side of her personality came out. She walked along, then stumbled over the castle, swinging her arms like windmills for balance, hopped forward twice, and then plopped backward right into the sand castle.

Petey, the dog, ran over, his leash trailing behind him, and gave her a big slurpy lick on the cheek. As a man with a big camera on his shoulder closed in on her face, Chloe wriggled her mouth into a funny line and looked up to the sky in exasperation. She had the crowd and the other actors in stitches.

"Excellent!" the director said, clearly thrilled. "That was exactly what I needed. Exactly!" He helped her to her feet, and they walked off together, talking. Again, I couldn't hear what he was saying. But when Chloe came jogging back to me, she had a big smile on her face.

"That was great," I said.

Chloe held out a card with writing on the back. "This is the director's card. He wants to know if I can be in some more scenes."

"Are you kidding?" I cried excitedly.

"No! He says he just got a brainstorm that I should be this mystery girl who bumps into things and stumbles over chairs and things like that through the whole show. Then Scooter—you know, the geeky character—develops a crush on me. This is the "Freshman Bell" two-hour summer special."

"Unbelievable!" I said.

"I told him I'd be busy with modeling and being in your movie, but he said they could work around me," Chloe said happily. "After he talks to the writers, he's going to call me tonight."

"That's awesome," I said. "You came out here to be an extra, and you're going home a star."

"I wouldn't say that." Chloe laughed. She checked her black plastic watch. "Whoa! Break is over. Let's go."

Life sure is funny, I thought as we jogged back to the spot where we were supposed to be modeling. Chloe got a break just by being in the right place at the right time. She was certainly having a different Hollywood experience than I was.

I decided to take a more positive approach. Acting was going to be fun. And it was going to be easy. I was determined to be a star.

Chapter Five

———◆———

Ashley, loosen up. You're way too stiff. Give us that model's ease, that self-confident stride. Become Julie," said Larry on the set later that same day. "Take a deep breath and start again."

I sucked in some air, but it didn't seem to help. I was trying so hard that I was just tensing up. I couldn't relax. We were working on a scene where Andrea invites Julie to a party, but only after every other kid in their class had been invited weeks earlier. Although Julie was really looking forward to the party, when she finds out she was invited as a sort of afterthought, her feelings are really hurt. She tells Andrea that she doesn't need her pity.

"This time, remember who you are, Ashley," said Larry. "You're a poor girl, and you're not sure if you fit in with these new kids."

"But I thought I was supposed to be self-confident," I objected.

"Normally you are, but you're in a strange situation now," Larry explained. "You're not worried about the kids liking you; you're not sure if you like them."

"Listen, Andrea," I began reading my line. "I don't need help from you or anybody."

Delia threw up her arms. "You sure need help from someone," she snapped.

That wasn't her line. She'd just insulted me.

Suddenly I'd had just about enough of her.

"Delia, I don't know what your problem is," I said angrily. "But if you don't get off my case, I'm going to pop you one."

"She threatened me!" Delia shouted at Larry.

"Well, you make me furious!" I shot back. As I shouted, I was dimly aware that something was going on around me. I looked over toward the door and saw that Johnny had come on the set. Even among the crew and other actors, he was a big deal. His show was in the top ten and getting more popular every week. Everyone was whispering, pointing, and gawking at him.

"All right, five-minute break!" Larry called in frustration. "Both you girls, go cool off."

Still shaking with anger, I went over to Johnny. "Ho, tiger!" he teased. "That girl really ticked you off, didn't she?"

"She's been on my case since I got here," I explained.

"I don't know why. I haven't done anything to her."

"Take a look at her and take a look at you," said Johnny. "You make her look like a homely twerp."

"*She's* the star," I objected.

"Yeah, and she doesn't want anyone to outshine her," Johnny said with a laugh.

"There's not much chance of that," I said sourly. "Did you see my scene? I was terrible!"

Johnny frowned thoughtfully. "The scene does need some work. But I had an idea that might help you. Do you remember how you yelled at Delia? You were great, really mad and full of fire. For a minute, I believed you really would pop her one."

"I'd sure like to," I said.

"So that's how you say those lines. Instead of saying, 'I don't know what your problem is, Delia,' say, 'Listen, Andrea, I don't need help from you or anybody.' Only say it with that same feeling, the same anger. Can you do that?"

I tried. I closed my eyes and pictured Delia's face. "Listen, Andrea, I don't need help from you or anybody!"

"Much better," said Johnny. "Keep in touch with your anger toward Delia when you do the scene. Transfer that anger to her character, Andrea."

When the break was up, I went back to try the scene again. "I hear that's your brother," Delia hissed at me. "Well, that explains why *you're* here."

I glared at her but didn't respond. I was staying in touch

with my anger. We began the scene, and this time when I spoke, I spat out the words angrily.

"Much, much better," Larry said at the end of the scene. "It still needs some shading to show different levels of feeling, but it's a great improvement. I think we're getting there."

I looked at Johnny and gave him a thumbs-up, which he returned with a smile.

Then, as I glanced over his shoulder, I saw a familiar figure step out of the shadows near a stack of mats the stunt people had brought in for a later scene.

It was my mother!

"Mom!" I cried, running to her. "When did you get back? How long have you been standing here?"

My mother hugged me. She looked as great as ever. Her blond hair was pulled back in a loose twist, and she had on a stylish beige pantsuit. There wasn't the slightest sign that she'd just spent weeks in a rain forest.

"I've been here from just before Johnny came in. I didn't want you to see me until your scene was over, because I didn't want to distract you," she said.

"Then you saw my scene?" I said excitedly. "What did you think?"

"The second was much better," said Mom. "Johnny is certainly a terrific acting coach. He really set you in the right direction."

I didn't ask about Johnny! What about me? I wanted to yell. But just then, Johnny joined us. He and Mom hugged warmly.

"Had enough of the rain forest?" he joked.

"No, it was fascinating, really. But I missed my children. With both of you on the West Coast, it didn't seem like I should be anywhere else."

"That's great, but what about your show?" I asked.

"There's a short break in the schedule. I have until the end of the week," she explained. "Then I'll have to go back."

"Come on, we're not done yet," I heard Larry yell.

"Are you free for dinner tonight?" Mom asked me.

"Well . . ." I hesitated. "Dad said he'd get home early and we'd barbecue. He's been so busy that this is actually the first night I'll be spending time with him."

"No problem," Mom said. "This is supposed to be your time with your father. How about lunch tomorrow?"

"I'll be here until noon, and at two o'clock I'll be modeling at the Azure Shores Hotel," I told her. "We could have lunch in between."

"Very good," said Mom. "I'll make a reservation for the three of us to have lunch in the hotel restaurant at twelve-thirty." She kissed my cheek. "I'll see you then, sweetheart. Good luck with the rest of the day."

She turned to go and Johnny ran after her. "See ya, Ashes," he called over his shoulder. "Don't worry. You're doing fine."

I wiggled my fingers at him. I wished I could have left, too. Instead I had to go back and do another scene with darling Delia.

By the time Cam picked me up outside the studio building, I was pretty frazzled. "You look worn-out, Miss Taylor," Cam observed politely. "Are you feeling well?"

"This acting business isn't as easy as it looks," I admitted wearily as I climbed into the backseat of the car. This was the first time Cam had ever said anything to me. I appreciated his concern.

As we were pulling out of the studio lot, the car phone buzzed. Cam picked it up. "Ted Hoffritz's line," he said. "Yes, she's right here."

Cam handed me the phone. It was Johnny. "Hi, Ashes, it's me. Listen, I know I said I'd help you with your lines tonight, but something's come up. Mom wants me to meet a director friend of hers. He's looking for an actor for his new movie. I really should meet him."

"Sure," I said. "It's okay. Dad and I are going to barbecue. He's finally got some free time."

"Great," said Johnny. "I'll catch you later."

"Later," I said, clicking off and handing the phone back to Cam. When we arrived at the house, my friends were already there. Nikki and Tracey were in the pool, but Chloe met me in the house. "How did it go?" she asked as I threw my straw bag on a chair.

"It was terrible at first, but then it got a little better," I told her. "I don't know, though. Maybe I'm not cut out to be an actress."

Chloe patted my shoulder. "You're just tense," she said.

"I'm sure you'll be great. Guess what? The guy from 'Freshman Bell' called already. They're going to write at least two new scenes for me. Isn't that great?"

"It sure is," I said. I went to shower. By the time I'd changed, I could smell steaks cooking on the grill. Finally I'd get to spend some time with Dad. I was really looking forward to it.

As I went down the hall, I thought I heard the sound of people talking. I heard laughter, too. When I got into the living room, I could see through the sliding glass doors. Out by the pool was a whole crowd of people I didn't know!

Dad had promised he'd make time for me tonight. What was going on?

Through the crowd, I saw Dad at the grill. I stormed out the door and headed right for him. When he saw me, his eyes lit happily. "Here she is!" he said for all to hear. "My daughter, Ashley, the star."

All eyes were on me. I had no choice but to turn my scowl to a smile. I waved at everyone. "Hi," I said.

"Take a good look at that beautiful face," Dad went on. "You'll be seeing a lot more of it. Ashley is starring in her first movie right now."

"How marvelous," said a beautiful woman in a short dress.

"Well, I'm not really the star," I said, embarrassed.

"She's the second lead, but she'll steal the movie," said Dad.

"Dad!" I pleaded. "Come on."

"You'll see," he insisted in front of everyone. "You've got star quality. I know about things like that."

Thank goodness, at that moment Mary appeared with a bowl of punch. "Help yourself, everyone," Dad said. "Steaks will be done in ten minutes or so."

The guests turned toward the punch bowl. "Who are all these people?" I whispered to Dad.

"They're the cast and crew of my movie," he explained. "Things were so tense on the set today that I had to do something to lighten the mood. So I invited everyone here for a barbecue. Have the waiters arrived yet?"

"What waiters?" I asked.

"I called an agency that provides extra help for parties," he explained.

"Dad, I thought we were going to spend some time together tonight," I complained.

"I know, hon, but I just had to do something," he said apologetically. "I knew you'd understand. We'll have some time another night. I promise."

"All right," I huffed. I was having a hard time being nice about this, I was so disappointed. "You shouldn't have told everyone I'm going to be a star."

"Why not? You *are* going to be a star."

"What if I'm not?" I asked.

"You will be," he said as he turned over a large steak on the grill. "I'm counting on it."

Suddenly a group of waiters in tuxedos arrived, looking like a flock of penguins. "Excuse me, Ashley," said Dad. "I have to tell these guys what to serve. Make sure these steaks don't burn."

As I watched him talk to the waiters, Nikki joined me. "Barbecues at my house are never like this," she said with a smile.

I found it hard to smile back. "So much for our quiet evening at home," I said, sighing.

Nikki put her hand on my shoulder. "There will be other nights."

"Yeah, sure," I said glumly.

Along with the cast and crew of Dad's movie, we had a wonderful dinner with steak, corn on the cob, and a huge salad. The waiters served everything and whisked away all the plates and glasses when we were done.

"Now, for your dancing pleasure, I've hired the hottest new group in town," Dad announced. At that, five guys in black T-shirts came out of the house carrying instruments. Where had Dad dug them up? He sure was a whiz at throwing together a last-minute bash.

The musicians began to play, and everyone started dancing. Dad danced with the beautiful actress in the short dress. He looked at me and waved. I forced a smile and waved back. Then I turned to Chloe, Nikki, and Tracey. "Let's get out of here," I said.

My friends and I went down to the beach for an

evening swim. "I'm having such a great time," said Nikki as we came out of the water together.

"It's pretty cool out here in California," agreed Tracey.

We all sat on a blanket. While the others talked, my mind wandered. I was thinking about the movie. What if I turned out to be a terrible actress, after all? What if I totally humiliated myself in this role? How could I face Dad? He was counting on me being a star! And what about Mom? I just couldn't disappoint her.

"What's wrong, Ashley?" Nikki asked me. "You look upset."

"I was just worrying about the movie," I admitted. "Did I tell you my mom showed up this afternoon?"

"She did? That was nice of her," said Chloe.

"It was," I said. "But somehow it makes me even more nervous."

"Why?" Nikki asked.

"I don't know. It's one more person judging me," I said.

"That's a funny way to look at it," said Nikki. "I'm sure she came to be supportive."

"And to make sure I don't goof up and embarrass her," I said. "I didn't need Dad telling everyone I'm going to be a star, either. Why couldn't he just have said, 'This is Ashley, my daughter'? Why wasn't that good enough?"

"Ashley," Chloe said slowly. "I think you're making yourself more tense than you have to be over this."

"What's that supposed to mean?" I asked, annoyed.

"This movie is a great chance and all, but your whole life isn't going to collapse if it doesn't go well," she said.

"How do you know?" I snapped, getting to my feet. "You don't know what's at stake here."

"You're right," Chloe said pointedly. "I don't know. What *is* at stake?"

How could I explain it? My position, my standing in my family was at stake. This was my chance to be equal with the rest of the achievers. "You wouldn't understand," I said. "I have to go. I'm supposed to learn my lines."

With that, I stomped off the beach, not exactly sure why I felt so angry.

Chapter Six

Thanks for going over my lines with me last night," I said to Nikki the next day as we walked into the studio. "Sorry I was such a crab."

"That's okay," said Nikki. "Remember how tense I was when I started modeling? It's scary at first when you try new things. But you helped me a lot. Besides, you weren't that crabby."

"Yes, I was," I said honestly. "I was in a bad mood to start with, and then I had so much trouble with those lines. I've never been good at memorizing."

Nikki had been a real pal. Despite my bad attitude, she'd sat up with me until past midnight reviewing the lines.

"Hey, guys! Wait up!" Tracey called to us. She and Chloe had stopped several yards back to stare at some of the stars from their favorite TV comedy. Now they hurried after us.

"This is so weird," said Tracey. "I feel like I'm walking around inside a TV set, watching the characters come to life."

"You do know that the characters are really actors, don't you?" Chloe asked her with a laugh.

"I suppose, but I don't think of them that way. To me, they're all just TV people. I wouldn't be surprised to see the Flintstones walking along out here."

Inside, the set was much more crowded than it had been the day before. All the cast was there, including the extras.

A classroom set had been built in a corner of the room. Lights were focused on it, and microphones hung from the ceiling.

"Okay, everybody!" shouted Dwight, Larry Morton's assistant. "We're going to run through and then see if we can get some film in the can today."

"What does that mean?" Nikki asked me.

"I don't know," I admitted. I saw Jack Jameson standing a few feet away and went over to him. "Did you understand what he just said?" I asked.

Jack smiled. "They want to go through a few scenes to make sure everyone knows the lines, and then they're going to try to do some filming."

"Today?" I yelped. "So soon?"

"Things go really fast on a TV movie," he said.

"No kidding," I said.

When Jack smiled, I noticed what really nice eyes he had. You could tell he was a nice person just by looking at his eyes. They were kind and happy. "Don't worry, you'll get the hang of things," he told me. "It just takes time."

"How much time?" I asked.

"By the time you do your second movie, you'll feel like an old pro," he assured me.

"If there ever is a second movie," I said skeptically.

"Someone with your looks will definitely do a second movie," said Jack.

That surprised me. I mean, I know I'm pretty—otherwise I wouldn't be a model. But it made me happy to hear Jack say it. "Thanks," I said.

Dwight read off a list of the student extras who would be seated in the classroom. Chloe, Tracey, and Nikki were all in my movie "class."

Larry came on the set. "Student extras, take your seats. Just grab a seat for today. We'll arrange you more carefully later on. We're doing act one, scene three right from the top."

Quickly I paged through my script. By now I knew most of the scenes, but I didn't remember what they were all called because we jumped around and didn't work on scenes in order.

I finally found my place. It was a scene where Julie reads her composition and some kids make wisecracks about it. I had a lot of lines in the scene. We'd rehearsed it yesterday, and it had gone all right. I was still nervous, though.

Yesterday I'd had the script in my hand and today I wouldn't. Besides that, this was the scene with the word *predilection* in it, which was still giving me trouble.

"Ashley, you'll sit here," Larry called to me, pointing toward one of the chairs. "Delia, you sit in the next row, right behind her. That way the camera can focus on both of you at once."

I took my place, not looking at Delia. I'd worked with difficult models before. I'd decided I could handle her the same way I handled them—by ignoring them and concentrating on what I was doing.

Amanda Michaels, the actress playing our teacher, took her place behind the teacher's desk. Nikki was able to grab the chair right behind mine.

"Okay," said Larry. "We're not filming, but if this works out, we'll go right to wardrobe and makeup, and then we'll do it. So make it good. From the top!"

Amanda spoke the opening lines. She was telling the class to read the compositions they'd written about their most remarkable relative.

In the scene, my character, Julie, reads a very interesting composition about her great-uncle who was a hobo and rode the rails back in the 1930s. Her essay tells all about the interesting things he saw and the offbeat life he led.

Anybody but a real clod would have been able to see that Julie's essay was great. Unfortunately a couple of her classmates *are* rich-kid clods, and they make fun of Julie's poor relative. The Andrea character isn't one of them, though. She's really impressed by Julie's essay, and she wants to get to know Julie better despite the fact that Julie doesn't fit in with Andrea's other friends. I suppose that's why the camera had to get her in while I was talking, so the audience could see her changing expression.

"All right, Julie. Let's hear from you," Amanda continued.

That was my cue to stand. Then I had to wait a moment for two other characters to make a crack about my clothing. When they were done, I was supposed to read my essay. Yesterday Larry told me not to really read it because that would sound too stiff. He wanted me to have it memorized.

"My most interesting relative was my great-uncle Jeb," I began. "He was a traveling salesman, but things didn't work out for him. During the Great Depression, no one had much money to buy anything, so Uncle Jeb stopped selling. But he didn't stop traveling, although he had to put aside his . . . his . . ."

"Predilection," Nikki whispered from behind me.

I wondered why she didn't have any trouble saying it.

"Proodle-duction," I said. "No, preed-dul-shon. No . . . uh . . ."

"Skip it. Keep going," Larry said.

"He had to put aside his *liking* of fast cars and trade it in for a new love—a love of riding the boxcars on the Yankee Spirit line. Uncle Jeb was a . . . a . . ." Suddenly my mind went blank. What was the next line?

As I tried desperately to come up with the words, I saw my mother walk onto the set, cool and star-like in a white jumpsuit.

Why had she picked that moment to show up? If I'd ever had any hope of remembering the next line, it was gone now. She'd thrown me completely off.

"Uncle Jeb was a man with a mission," Nikki whispered from behind me.

"A . . . a . . . man with a mission," I said. But then I went blank once more.

"He was on a personal journey of discovery," Nikki coached.

"He was on a personal journal of discovery," I parroted her.

"He was out to discover the real America," Nikki prompted me in a loud whisper.

Again I repeated the line.

"Give me a break," Delia muttered, loud enough so everyone could hear.

"Ashley," Larry broke in. "Did you study the lines?"

"Sure I did," I said.

"Well, your girlfriend seems to know them better than you do," he said irritably. "Maybe *she* should play the part of Julie."

I whirled around and looked at Nikki, who was cringing. Behind her, Chloe and Tracey were staring down at their folded hands.

"Maybe she should!" I shouted angrily, tears springing to my eyes. If Larry didn't want me there, I sure wasn't going to force myself on him. Not wanting to cry in front of everyone, I ran from the set toward the door.

Just as I was about to push open the door, a hand caught me firmly around my upper arm. I looked up and gazed right into my mother's striking blue eyes. "Where are you going, Ashley?" she asked in a soft but forceful tone of voice.

"Out of here," I said, the tears spilling over now.

"No, you're not," said Mom. "Did I raise a quitter?"

"Mo-om!" I wailed.

"Ashley, you've been a professional model all your life. What does Kate Calico always say?"

"A Calico model gets the job done." I recited the words I'd heard a zillion times. "She's the epitome of the true professional."

"That little outburst was pretty unprofessional," Mom pointed out.

A quick glance back at the set told me Larry had called a break. "But he wants Nikki for the role," I protested.

"No, he doesn't," Mom disagreed. "He wants you to have your lines memorized so he can film and keep to his schedule. I think you owe him an apology."

"Really? Don't you think that's going overboard?" I asked, reluctant.

"Not for a professional."

I sighed deeply. If my mother was anything, it was professional. She knew what she was talking about. "All right," I said dismally. "I'll apologize."

"That's my girl," said Mom.

I spotted Larry across the room and walked over to him. "I'm sorry," I said. "I shouldn't have blown up like that."

"I can live with blowups," he said. "I can't live with actresses who don't know their lines. We can't go forward unless you know your lines."

"I'm sorry," I said. "I know most of them."

"Good. Now learn the rest of them," he said.

"I will," I assured him.

As I walked back to get my script, I saw Tracey, Chloe, and Nikki huddled together, looking worried. Nikki rushed up to me. "I'm so sorry," she said. "I was only trying to help. Honestly."

"How did you know all the lines?" I asked her.

"I remembered them from last night. I've always been good at memorizing."

"Maybe you *should* be playing Julie," I said.

"No, he didn't mean that," said Nikki. "I would be terrible in the part. I'm not an actress."

I looked at her. Then I looked at my mother, who was talking to someone she knew. "Maybe I'm not an actress, either," I said.

Chapter Seven

——◆——

Mom and I didn't talk much on the ride over to the Azure Shores Hotel. She could see I was in a bad mood. Larry had told me to use the script for the rest of the rehearsals. Because of me, he didn't get to film any of the scenes I was in. I also felt like a fool being the only one with a script in my hand.

In the backseat, Tracey, Nikki, and Chloe chattered constantly. "This should be the last day of the photo shoot, don't you think?" said Nikki.

"I hope so," said Chloe, "because I told the 'Freshman Bell' people I'd be free tomorrow morning. You know, I've appeared in so many ads, but when I called home and said I'd be on TV, my family went wild."

"My mother is still impressed that I'm a model," said

Tracey. "She has all my ads hanging in her office at work. It's pretty embarrassing."

"My parents actually have mine *framed*!" Nikki laughed.

"I framed Ashley's modeling pictures when she was a baby," said my mother as she steered her rented car into the driveway of the hotel. "But after a while, I had so many of them that I stopped doing that."

I wasn't even sure if Mom had all my modeling pictures anymore. I guess they just didn't impress her. I knew she had a scrapbook of Johnny's press clippings, though. His being a big TV star impressed her.

She parked, and we headed for the grand front door with its blue-striped awning. "Would you girls like to join us for lunch?" Mom offered.

"No, thanks," said Nikki. "We're going to jump into the pool while we have the chance."

Inside, Nikki, Chloe, and Tracey went to the left, and Mom and I went to the right. "See you guys down on the beach at two," I said, waving.

"We'll be by the pool if you finish lunch early," said Nikki.

When they were out of earshot, Mom said, "I didn't mean to embarrass you today by making you apologize. I only wanted you to do the right thing. I hope you understand that, Ashley."

"I wasn't embarrassed," I told her. "You were right. But, you know, Mom, I did study the lines. My mind just went blank."

"Some people memorize better than others. I never had any trouble with that. Neither does Johnny. But you're different. So you have to work a little harder at it. That's all."

As I listened to my mother, I tried to imagine her speaking in a whispery voice with a slight lisp. I couldn't. "Mom, does my voice sound all right?" I asked her as we walked into the elegant green and blue hotel dining room.

"Work on the sibilant *s*, and you'll be fine," she said.

"The what?" I asked.

"Sibilant," she repeated. "It means you make a hissing sound. Too many *s* sounds in a sentence can make you sound like a snake hissing. It's very unpleasant."

Great! I had just discovered that my mother thought I sounded like a snake. How much worse could this day get? "Do you think I need a speech coach?" I asked.

"It might be a good idea," she replied. That proved it!

We spotted Johnny seated and waiting for us in the dining room. He appeared every inch the star, his tan looking extra deep against his crisp white shirt. "Hi," he said when we joined him. "I'm glad you finally got here. I'm starving."

"When are you *not* starving?" Mom laughed. "And you never gain a pound."

"Neither do I," I said, taking my seat.

"Well, you don't eat like a horse," said Mom.

We'd just opened our menus when a tall, balding man came up to our table. I'd never seen him before, but Mom and Johnny both seemed to get tense as soon as he arrived.

"My, my, what a picture this makes," he said with a big, phony smile. "Taylor Andrews and her heartthrob son, Johnny Renee."

"Hello, Mr. Wilcox," Mom said in a voice that was icy yet polite. "Yes, indeed, you've spotted us. There's no hiding from you, is there?"

That's when I remembered who this guy was. Mom had complained about him before. He was one of the most well-known celebrity photographers around—and the pushiest. He followed famous people everywhere, hounding them until he got the pictures he wanted.

"Who is this young lady with you?" he asked.

"This is my daughter, Ashley," Mom said.

Mr. Wilcox squinted his eyes as he looked at me. He was probably trying to remember if he'd ever seen me on TV. "Come on, Taylor. How about a shot of you and your famous kid?"

"Kids," Mom corrected. "I suppose that would be all right. As long as it doesn't take long."

"Sure thing," he agreed. "I just need you and Johnny to stand over here."

Mom and Johnny stood by the window Mr. Wilcox pointed to. "Ashley, come on," said Mom.

Mr. Wilcox looked at me quickly. His frown told me he didn't want me in the picture. He didn't consider me famous enough. "It's okay," I said, staying seated.

"Don't be shy, Ashes," said Johnny.

"Yes, of course, come on," said Mr. Wilcox. His smile was forced, and his darting eyes and uneasy voice told me he wasn't sincere. He was just trying to keep Mom and Johnny happy.

I didn't know what else to do, so I got up and stood by Mom. "Very good," said Mr. Wilcox. "Young lady, you sit in front of your mother, all right?" I pulled up a chair, and Mr. Wilcox started snapping pictures. But I got the feeling he was shooting over my head. After all, I'd had my picture taken a zillion times. I knew what a camera looked like when it was aimed at me. This one wasn't.

"Now, how about a picture of all of you in the entryway?" Mr. Wilcox suggested.

"All right," Mom agreed. "But that's the last."

"Sure, sure," said Mr. Wilcox as we walked to the doorway of the dining room.

"Taylor, Johnny, you stand with your arms around each other," Mr. Wilcox directed. "Ashley, you stand a few feet to the right. That will make a good composition."

"I think Ashley should stand beside us," Mom said in her firm, this-is-a-polite-order voice.

"No, trust me. This will look better," Mr. Wilcox disagreed.

"No way," said Johnny. "Ashes, come over here." I was sure Mr. Wilcox was trying to cut me out of the photos. Even Johnny and Mom could see what was going on now.

"It's okay," I said. "He doesn't really want me in the photo."

"Of course he does," Mom insisted.

"Taylor, why don't I get a few of you and Johnny and then some with all of you together," Mr. Wilcox suggested cagily. I knew where the photos with me would end up—in the garbage.

"Forget it," I said. "I don't want to be anywhere I'm not wanted."

"Ashley!" Mom said sharply. I knew she was thinking that I was throwing another tantrum. I couldn't help it, though. My feelings were hurt.

"If the young lady doesn't want to be in the photo, we shouldn't force her," Mr. Wilcox said too eagerly.

"See?" I said. "He doesn't want me!"

"No offense, young lady. But I only photograph famous people. And I've never heard of you."

"You will," Johnny said angrily.

"Well, until I do, I don't really need her picture," replied Mr. Wilcox.

"Ignore him," Johnny said to me. "Hey, Wilcox, why don't you get lost?"

"I don't take orders from punks," the photographer shot back angrily. "Guys like me can make or break flash-in-the-pan guys like you."

With that, Johnny stepped toward him with his fist clenched. "Johnny, please," my mother said. "This is what he wants. He'll sell the picture of you swinging at him to every cheap tabloid in town."

But Johnny was mad now. He started to walk toward the photographer. As he did, Mr. Wilcox started snapping pictures. The more pictures he shot, the angrier Johnny got.

If he hit the photographer, it would be big news. It might really hurt his career.

Everyone in the dining room was staring at us. From across the room, I saw the maître d' rushing our way.

"Forget it!" I said. Tears were brimming in my eyes. I didn't want anyone to see me cry. "I'll leave. Let him have his picture. It's no big deal."

"You stay right here, Ashes," Johnny said, glowering at Mr. Wilcox.

I couldn't stay, though. It was all so mortifying. "Let her have a minute alone," I heard Mom tell Johnny as I rushed out of the dining room.

I stood in the lobby of the hotel, breathing hard with anger. Boy, did I ever feel like a big nobody! Even a sleazeball photographer like that Wilcox guy didn't want my picture.

As I stood there, I noticed that the newsstand across the lobby was featuring the new issue of *Teen World*—the one with me on the front cover. I went to the stand and picked the magazine off the front rack. I was modeling a western-style outfit—flounced denim skirt, an embroidered, fringed shirt, red cowboy boots, and a cowboy hat. I was smiling brightly.

I felt like charging back into the dining room and shoving the magazine in Wilcox's face. But I just wasn't ready to go back in there. Still, seeing the picture made me feel better. I wasn't a nobody. I was a top model on the cover of a major magazine.

Just then someone placed a hand on my shoulder. I turned sharply. "Is that you?" asked Jack Jameson.

"Hi," I said, surprised to see him. "Yes, this is me."

"Wow!" he said, taking the magazine from me. "You look great."

"Thanks," I said. "What are you doing here?"

Jack looked embarrassed. "I had an interview with a reporter. She's in from New York, and she wants to write something about me for her magazine."

"How cool!" I said. "You're going to be a hot young heartthrob!"

Jack blushed. "It's really stupid."

"No, it's not," I said. "It's great. My mom says that good publicity makes careers."

"She should know, I guess," he said with a pleasant smile. "I mean, I know she's Taylor Andrews from what Delia said."

I rolled my eyes. "Don't remind me of Delia. I'm having a bad enough day."

"Delia's a jerk," Jack said, dismissing the subject. "She's just jealous of you."

"Think so?" I asked.

"Sure." He tapped the magazine. "Look at you. Wouldn't you be jealous if you were her? I didn't know you were such a successful model."

"I do all right," I said modestly.

"You sure do," he agreed. "I bet you'll be a big movie star once you get the hang of it."

"You, too," I said. I thought that would make him happy, but instead he frowned. "Don't you want to be a movie star?" I asked.

"I wouldn't mind if it just kind of happened," he said with a smile. "Then I'd have enough money to be a vet, which is what I'd really like to do. It's weird. All this movie stuff just sort of happened to me. I didn't choose it. But how can you turn down being a movie star? It's what everyone wants. So I'll work on it and see what happens. How about you? Do you want to be a movie star?"

I nodded. "I'm going to be one, too. That probably sounds pretty unbelievable to you after what happened today on the set."

"No, it's not unbelievable," said Jack. "You're lucky to be so sure of what you want."

"I suppose," I said.

"I'd better go," said Jack. "I'm supposed to see one more reporter. She's interviewing me about the movie we're doing. Want me to mention you?"

"Why not?" I said. "But only if you say good things."

Jack smiled and gave me a thumbs-up. "See you," he said.

Just as he disappeared through a set of swinging doors, I saw Wilcox charging out of the dining room. My mother and Johnny were right behind him. "Oh, there you are, Ashley," said my mother. "Are you all right?"

"Sure," I said.

"I'm sorry about that," she said. "He's just so pushy."

"He's lucky I didn't punch him," Johnny snarled.

"No, *you're* lucky you didn't punch him," my mother disagreed heatedly. "It would not have helped your career at all."

"Sometimes you just have to forget about your career," said Johnny, still angry.

Mom took his arm and steered him back toward the dining room. "No, you must never forget about your career. It's what you've worked hard for. Now come on, let's eat."

I followed my mother and Johnny into the dining room. Talking to Jack had made me feel better. But that good feeling was fading. Standing between Mom and Johnny was making me feel very small and unimportant all over again.

Chapter Eight

——◆——

How many more pictures do you need?" I moaned to Stefan, the photographer. We'd been posing on the beach all afternoon.

I'd modeled more bathing suits, rompers, sweats, and sundresses than I could ever have imagined possible. The sand seemed to be getting into every pore of my skin, and I'd applied so much sunblock that I was as slippery as an eel. I just wanted to go home, pull the sheets over my head, and forget all about this day.

"Do you want to have to come back tomorrow?" Stefan asked as he popped yet another roll of film into his camera.

"No!" all four of us answered at once.

"Then, just a few more minutes." A few more minutes

turned into a half hour, but finally he was done. "Thank you, ladies," he said. "I think we have enough."

"Whew!" said Tracey, pushing her dark hair away from her face and putting on her sunglasses. "My face hurts from smiling."

"Mine, too," Chloe agreed, stretching.

As we sat on the sand, we saw Gloria, the company representative, scurrying across the beach toward us.

"All done?" she asked cheerfully. We all nodded wearily. "Stefan, did you get any pictures by the pool?"

Stefan's face fell. "No. I didn't know you wanted any," he said.

"Oh, yes, we want that resort feeling. This isn't just beachwear," she replied.

Groaning, we all got up and began trudging toward the pool. "Sorry, girls," Stefan said.

All together, in dull voices, we recited Kate Calico's motto. "The Calico model always gets the job done. She is the epitome of professionalism." Kate would be proud of us, but I was exhausted.

When we got to the pool, Delia Carrol was lounging there in a hot pink two-piece suit. She was about the last person I wanted to see just then.

She looked up and rolled her eyes when she saw me. "Working hard on memorizing your lines, I see," she said smugly. "I guess we can forget about shooting anything tomorrow, too."

"Don't worry about me. What are *you* doing here?" I snapped.

"Mother and I stay here when I'm filming," she replied haughtily. "Is that all right with you?"

"Ignore her," Chloe said.

I tried, but it would be hard to smile naturally for Stefan's camera with Delia's beady little eyes trained on me. I felt like she was just waiting for me to do something stupid so she could comment.

"All right," said Stefan. "If they want pool, we'll give them pool." He shot pictures of Chloe and Nikki by the pool, dressed in their bathing suits. Meanwhile, he sent Tracey and me to the hotel room to change into sundresses.

The dresses were pretty, with floral patterns, cap sleeves, and gathered waists. Mine came with a wide-brimmed straw hat with a matching band.

"I hope no one sees me in this thing," said Tracey as she strained to zip the back. "I don't believe I have to put it on *again.*"

"Let me do that for you," I said, coming up behind her and zipping the dress. "I know this isn't your style, but you look great." The purple and green irises on a cream-colored background looked striking with Tracey's aqua eyes.

My dress was covered with red and pink roses and had a wide lace collar. I loved it. The dresses were super feminine, which was why Tracey hated them.

"This frilly stuff isn't me," she said. "I feel like a total dweeb."

I looked at Tracey a moment. "I admire that about you," I said sincerely.

"What? That I have the ability to feel like a total dweeb?"

"No, silly, that you know who you are. You know what you like and what you want."

"Don't you?" she asked. "You seem as if you do."

"I used to," I said. "Lately I'm not so sure."

"Well, I don't always know who I am, but I know who I'm not. I'm not a person who would ever wear this dress," she said, flapping the skirt helplessly.

"Come on," I said with a smile. "The faster we get out there, the faster you can take it off."

We returned to the pool just as Chloe and Nikki were getting out. "All right, girls," Stefan said to us. "Stand right on the edge of the pool and put your arms around each other as if you're sisters or cousins or something. Then I want big, happy smiles. Pretend you're on your way to a garden party."

"Gross me out," Tracey whispered through her smile as we got into position.

"Should I hold the hat?" I asked.

"No, wear it," Stefan said. "We might as well go all out with the look."

I placed the hat on my head, adjusting the elastic strap in the back, and put my arm around Tracey's shoulder. We stood there like that, smiling for what seemed a very long time. Stefan kept looking into his camera but not taking a picture. "What's wrong?" I asked finally.

"Something isn't working," he said. He went over to a table by the pool and plucked a bouquet of flowers from a tall vase. "Here," he said, handing them to me. "Hold these flowers. It will add some pizzazz to the photo."

"I feel like I just won a beauty pageant," I said as I held the tall flowers in my arms.

"You look so sweet, I'm getting a toothache," Tracey teased.

"You both look beautiful," said Nikki from the side, where she and Chloe sat wrapped in towels.

"The picture still isn't right," Stefan said. "Maybe it's the color pattern. You guys clash somehow."

"I'll leave," Tracey immediately volunteered.

"No, you stay," said Stefan. "Chloe, go get a different dress and replace Ashley."

"Good thinking," said Delia, who had come closer to watch. She stood there acting so smug and superior, her arms folded, her right hip slung forward.

"Look, Delia," I said sharply, turning toward her. But as I turned, I shifted my weight back and moved my foot a little. The next thing I knew, my feet were slipping out from under me, and I was hurtling backward into the pool!

Even as I flapped my arms in a hopeless attempt to right myself, I could hear Delia's shrill laughter ringing in my ears.

And then all I heard was the gurgly quiet of being underwater.

Sputtering, I came up for air. My hat was slung forward on the front of my head. The elastic band had gotten tangled in my hair. When I tried to pull it off, the hat snapped back and sent a torrent of water right into my face. All around me, flowers floated.

Delia was laughing as if her sides would split at any moment. The shrill, horrible sound seemed to fill the air.

In the next second, I was distracted from her by a horrifying sight. Mr. Wilcox, the obnoxious photographer, was standing at the pool's edge taking picture after picture—of me!

"Hi, again," he called. "Nothing like a little publicity to help a budding career."

"She needs all the help she can get," Delia added, still laughing.

"Hey, stop that!" Tracey yelled at Mr. Wilcox.

All I could do was drag myself out of the pool, my dress soaked, my ridiculous hat dripping water in my face, and the mascara I always wore when I was modeling running down my cheeks.

I wasn't going to give that Wilcox guy a chance to take another picture. And I couldn't listen to Delia's laughter a second more. Feeling like the biggest loser on earth, I turned and ran away from the pool, down the steps, and along the path. I didn't know where I was going, only that I wanted to get away from everybody and everything.

I was so blinded by the tears in my eyes that I didn't see the boy wheeling his bike onto the path. I crashed right into him, knocking us both to the ground. When I looked up, I saw it was Jack.

"Ashley!" he cried in surprise. "What's wrong?"

I was crying so hard that I couldn't answer him.

"Can I help?" Jack asked.

"Yes, give me a ride out of here right now."

He stood, righted his bike, and gave me a hand up. "Hop on," he said. "We're outta here."

Chapter Nine

———◆———

Where are we going?" I asked Jack when he stopped for a traffic light.

"I was going home. Is there somewhere in particular you want to go?"

"No," I said.

"Then let's go to my house."

"Okay."

He rode on, turning off the main road to a suburban area where the neat houses were pretty close together. After ten more minutes, he pedaled up the driveway of a plain white house.

Climbing off the bike, I remembered how I looked—soaking wet, mascara dripping down my face, my hair all stringy, the stupid hat still stuck to my head. I wasn't exactly in the best condition to meet his family. "Is anyone home?" I asked. "I'm kind of a mess."

As I spoke, I worked on getting that elastic band out of my hair. With a snap, it finally came loose.

"My parents might be home by now," said Jack. "I'm not sure if my sister is. We'll go in the back door, and you can duck right into the bathroom, if you want."

"All right," I agreed.

"Don't worry about how you look," he said as we went around to the back of the house. "My parents aren't fussy. Besides, you look pretty good for someone who just fell into a pool and crashed into a bike."

"Thanks." I laughed.

We went in the door, and I stepped right into the small bathroom on the right. I washed my face and used some cream I found on a shelf to get rid of the last of the mascara. Then I ran a comb through my tangled hair.

There was a knock on the door, and I opened it. "These are my sister's," said Jack, handing me a pair of lightweight sweats and a T-shirt. "She won't mind if you borrow them."

I took the clothing from him and put it on. The pants were a little large, but I didn't care. It was so good to get out of that damp dress.

When I stepped out of the bathroom, Jack was in the kitchen pouring two sodas. "I feel a lot better. Thanks," I said.

"No problem," he said, handing me a glass. "What happened?"

I explained why I'd been so upset. "So this ridiculous picture of me, soaking wet and furious, is going to be in the papers." I plopped into a kitchen chair. "Gee, I thought it was bad when I was just a nobody. Now I'm an attention-getting starlet. That's even worse."

"But *you* know that's not true," Jack pointed out.

"I know," I said. "I've embarrassed my parents, though."

"You didn't do anything embarrassing. You just slipped," Jack reminded me. "It could have happened to anyone."

"I know, but it happened to me. That's different from it happening to just anyone," I argued.

"Why?"

"Because I'm Taylor Andrews' daughter and Johnny Renee's sister. And to people in Hollywood, it will matter that I'm Ted Hoffritz's daughter, since he's well-known here. I've disgraced myself and my whole family."

Jack burst out laughing.

"What's so funny?" I demanded.

"Disgraced your family? That sounds like we're in the Middle Ages or something. 'Oh, it's so dreadful. I fell in the pool and disgraced my family!'"

That made me smile. It did sound pretty dumb. "It's more than that, though. I'm not measuring up as an actress, either."

Jack sat down and looked at me thoughtfully. "What happens if you really blow it, big time?" he asked.

"Oh, please. I change my name and move to some far-off country. Maybe I can find a plastic surgeon to give me a new face."

"Seriously," Jack said, grinning. "What would really happen?"

"I don't know. Nothing would happen, but I'd feel terrible."

"Would you get over feeling terrible after a while?" he asked.

"I suppose."

"So it wouldn't really be a tragedy or anything," he suggested.

"That's where you're wrong," I argued. "It *would* be a tragedy. Don't you think it's a tragedy to be the least-talented person in your family?"

Just then the back door opened, and a young woman came in. She was probably about twenty-one, and she was simply dressed in slacks and a beige shirt. Her blond hair was combed back in a French braid. I noticed that her wide blue eyes were the same as Jack's. "Hi," she said cheerfully.

"This is my sister, Samantha," said Jack. "Sammi, this is Ashley. She's in the movie, too. She sort of fell into a pool, so I lent her some of your clothes."

Samantha smiled. "That's okay. Hi, Ashley."

"Hi," I said.

"How did it go today?" Jack asked her.

"Class was almost empty. A lot of the students left before break to go skiing in Colorado."

"Sammi studies painting at the Smith-Watson Institute," Jack told me. I'd heard of the institute. It was a top art school with a great reputation. I also knew it was very expensive.

"I got a scholarship," she explained, as if she was reading my thoughts.

"Do you like it?" I asked.

"I love it," she said, pulling open the refrigerator door.

"She won the school's biggest award in her first year," Jack said proudly. "Want to see some of her paintings?" he asked me.

"Sure," I said. I followed him out of the kitchen and into the living room. On the wall were two beautiful seascapes. "Are these hers?" I asked.

"Yeah. She's good, isn't she?" said Jack.

"She is. It's nice that you're so proud of her."

"Sure, I'm proud of her," he said. "She's worked really hard, and she didn't let those snobby rich kids get to her. Some of them made her feel like a real outsider at first."

I continued looking around the neat, simple living room. On the wall near the door was a piece of embroidery in a frame. The embroidered words said "You Are Special!"

Unexpectedly the words brought tears to my eyes.

"What's wrong?" Jack asked me.

I quickly wiped away the tears. "It must be nice to be somebody special," I said.

"Oh, that," said Jack. "My mother embroiders. That's one of her favorite sayings. She's always repeating it to us."

"She is?"

"She says we're special because we're her kids." Jack laughed. "She's easy to please in that way. She thinks we're great no matter what."

"You're lucky," I said sincerely.

"Want to take a walk?" Jack asked after a moment.

"Okay." We went outside and began walking down the block.

"You know, at first Sammi couldn't see that she was every bit as good—even better—than most of the students at Smith-Watson," Jack said. "Still, she hung in there, and now she's considered one of the best students in her class. But she's not studying art to be famous. She's just doing what she loves to do."

We walked a block without saying anything. "That wouldn't work in my family," I said after a while. "In my family, you have to be famous to be somebody."

"Do your parents really feel that way, or is that how you feel?" Jack asked.

His question made me stop walking. Where *had* I gotten the idea that they felt that way? Was it from the way they fussed over Johnny? Or did I think my mother had started me modeling as a baby because she expected me to be famous? Was it that I wanted to be like the rest of my family? Or was *I* the one who was afraid to be different?

"What if you were a great scientist and made great contributions to humanity, but no one knew about you. Would your family be proud of you?"

"I don't know," I admitted.

"Or suppose you decided to be a gardener because you loved gardening. What if that was the thing that made you really happy. What would your parents think of you then?" he asked.

I shrugged. I just didn't know.

But maybe it was time I found out.

Chapter Ten

—◆—

Do you want to stay for supper?" Jack asked me when we returned from our walk about an hour later.

I wasn't sure if I should. I didn't want my family and friends to worry about me. But I really didn't feel like going back yet, either.

Just then the roar of a motorcycle engine made Jack and me turn. I looked down the dusky road at the approaching motorcycle. "It's my brother!" I said.

Johnny pulled up in front of Jack's house. "Ashley," he said as he pushed back his helmet, "are you okay?"

"I'm feeling better," I told him. "What are you doing here?"

"Chloe saw you leave with Jack," he explained. "I

looked in the phone book." He held up a page he'd torn out. "I've been checking the addresses of anyone named Jameson for the past two hours."

"Why?" I asked.

"Why?" he yelled. "Because I was worried about you, that's why. I told Cam I'd pick you guys up, but when I got to the hotel I found your friends in an uproar, all worried about you. I drove them all to Dad's, then took my bike out to look for you."

"Did they tell you what happened?" I asked.

"Yeah, they told me," he said. "I should have punched Wilcox this afternoon when I had the chance." He unstrapped an extra helmet from the back of his motorcycle. "Come on. Hop on."

"Thanks, Jack," I said, turning back to him. "I guess I'll see you tomorrow."

"So long," he said. "I hope you feel better."

"Thanks for looking after my sister," Johnny said to Jack as I climbed on the back of Johnny's motorcycle. Jack waved and then walked up to his house.

"He seems like a good guy," Johnny commented.

I took the helmet from him. "He's really nice," I agreed. "Johnny, I'm not ready to go home yet. Do you think we could just sort of ride around or something? Would you mind?"

"No problem," he said, and then revved the motor. We zoomed down the street and onto the main road.

I'd been on Johnny's motorcycle before. I loved the speed and the feeling of the breeze swooshing by. I hung on tight and let my mind go blank.

Johnny turned up a hilly street. The road curved sharply as we drove along, and it was a little scary in spots, but the view was gorgeous. The vastness of the rolling hills below—bathed in the oranges and pinks of the setting sun—made me feel my problems weren't as immense as I'd thought.

After about a half hour, we began to go down the other side of the hill. At the base of the hill, the ocean came into view, all sparkly and gold. Johnny rode into the parking lot of a big wooden building. A sign on the roof read SID'S SEAFOOD. Johnny parked and turned off the engine.

"Hungry?" he asked.

"Starving," I replied, suddenly realizing that my stomach was rumbling. We went inside, and Johnny ordered breaded shrimp, French fries, fried clams, coleslaw, and two large sodas. The food came in red-checked cardboard bowls on a cardboard tray. Johnny carried the tray out the side door, where five picnic tables were clustered together.

We were the only people there. We sat at a table and began to eat. "Ashes," Johnny said, "what's bugging you?"

I stirred a fry around in the puddle of ketchup I'd made. "Ever since I came out here, I feel like a failure. But you're a big success. You're someone Mom and Dad can be proud of. I'm just an embarrassment."

There, it was out. I'd said it.

"You're crazy," Johnny said.

I looked up at him sharply. "What do you mean?"

"They're proud of you, too. In fact, you can't do anything wrong. I'm constantly messing up in one way or another."

"You?" I cried. "No way!"

"Yes way! I'm always doing something like almost getting into a fistfight with that Wilcox guy this afternoon. Mom really chewed me out for that."

"She did?"

"Oh, yeah. She said it was totally unprofessional and she'd seen too many hotheads ruin their careers that way. You know how Mom is—a fanatic about being professional."

"Do I ever know it!" I laughed. "It's like being a professional is the only thing that's important to her. She's even worse than Kate Calico. It's all she thinks about."

"I used to think that, too," Johnny said as he picked at his shrimp. "But then I figured it out. She's worked so hard to get the career she has, and she loves her career so much, that she wants us to have it easier. She's trying to give us the head start she'd have liked."

"I suppose so," I said thoughtfully. When I looked at it the way Johnny did, it made sense. It even explained why she'd taken me to be a model as a baby—to give me a head start. "How did you figure that out?" I asked.

"Why else would she try so hard for us? You know, when I moved out here, she could have been mad at me, but she wasn't. She just tried to steer me in the right direction and help me make a success of my acting."

"But what if you didn't want to be an actor?" I questioned him.

"Don't you want to be one?" Johnny asked.

"I'm not sure," I admitted openly for the very first time.

"What about being a model?" he asked. "Don't you like that?"

"I love being a model. It's great," I said.

"Do you like it better than acting?"

"Yes," I said. "So far it's no contest."

"Then do it," said Johnny. "Model and forget about acting."

"What would Mom think?"

"What would you think?" he asked. "No, forget what you'd think. How would you feel?"

"I'd feel happy. I'm happy when I'm modeling."

"So what else is important?"

"But what about Mom and Dad?"

"They'd still be your parents. They wouldn't disown you or anything like that."

"I wouldn't have their respect," I said.

"You'd have your own respect," said Johnny. "And I think you'd have theirs, too. You have mine, no matter what."

It was the first time I'd ever talked to Johnny like this. There was such a big age difference between us that we'd never talked really seriously before. Up until now, Johnny had just treated me like his cute little sister—sweet, but not somebody to take too seriously.

"Look, Ashes, you may think I've got it all, but I admire you," Johnny continued. "You're gutsy. You came out here like a champ and tried out for the part without a single acting lesson. You got it, too. You stood up to Delia Carrol, who is well-known for being a first-class brat. You're going to do all right in life no matter what you decide to do. Anybody can see that."

"Yeah?" I asked, pleased.

"Yeah," he said. "You don't have anything to worry about."

"I feel a lot better," I said honestly. "I guess I've been acting like a jerk."

"That's okay," Johnny said. "Everybody gets to act like a jerk once in a while."

We finished eating and got back on the motorcycle. "Are you ready to go home now?" Johnny asked.

"Yes," I said. "Let's go." We rode home in silence as the dusk turned to darkness. "I hope everyone isn't too worried," I said when we pulled into the driveway.

Johnny shrugged as he turned off his motorcycle. "I guess you'll find out."

I climbed the stone steps that sloped gently up to the back of Dad's house, near the pool. It was completely dark, but I could see patio lights twinkling. By the time I hit the top step, I heard the sound of voices. "Here she comes," Chloe was saying in a loud whisper.

As soon as I stepped onto the patio, I saw a banner that read: ASHLEY, WE LOVE YOU! CHEER UP! Then Chloe, Nikki, and Tracey stepped out from behind the cabana. "We love you, Ashley, oh yes we do. We love you, Ashley, we do! Oh, Ashley, we love you!" they sang out.

"This is Cheer Up Ashley Night!" Chloe announced.

Nikki and Tracey pulled up a lounge chair. "Sit, your highness." Nikki giggled. "This is your night."

"You guys." I laughed as I took my seat. "You don't have to do this."

"Sure we do," said Chloe. "You've had a terrible day. What are friends for?"

Tracey presented me with a straw and a tall glass full of something red and fruity-looking. "A strawberry shake made with fresh strawberries, pineapple juice, and ginger ale," she explained.

"We've also planned an ice cream sundae-making extravaganza for later," said Nikki. "But first, a presentation." Nikki took a straw hat from under a table. "In this hat, we have placed slips of paper listing the top five great things about Ashley Taylor," she said as if she was the announcer on a game show. She handed the hat to me. I could see folded slips of pink paper inside. "Take one, please," she said.

I picked a piece of paper from the hat and unfolded it. "Considering how good-looking you are, you're not nearly as conceited as I would have expected," I read. "Well, thanks a lot, Tracey." I laughed.

"How did you know I wrote that one?" she asked, her hands on her hips.

"Who else would write something like this?" I asked with a smile. "But I appreciate it. Does it mean I'm sort of conceited?"

"It means what it says," said Tracey. "You have a right to be very conceited, but you're not."

"Pick another," Chloe urged me.

I took another slip from the hat. "You are a generous person," I read. I knew it wasn't Chloe's handwriting, and it wasn't Tracey's, either. It had to be from Nikki. "But I've never given you anything, Nikki," I said.

"I don't mean things," Nikki said. "I meant you're generous with yourself and what you know. When I first got to the agency, I was scared to death. You were friendly to me and made me feel at home. From the very start, you've shared everything you know with me."

"Anyone would have done that," I objected.

"That's not so," said Chloe. "Look how Delia has been

treating you. She hasn't exactly been generous."

"That's true," I had to admit. "Well, I was glad to do it. You're a nice person."

"So are you," said Nikki.

I took out another slip. "Nobody pushes you around. You have guts."

"Thanks, Tracey," I said. Then I picked another. "You're a fun person." I looked at Nikki and smiled. The last slip was written in Chloe's loopy writing. "You are the very best best friend anyone could ever hope for."

"That's the truth," Chloe said.

"The same goes for you," I agreed. "Thanks, you guys. You've made me feel much better."

"You may not feel that way after you see what these guys have planned next," said Tracey. Chloe and Nikki were busy spreading out the mat from my Twister game. On each of the colored circles they were placing cake pans filled with colored Jell-O.

"This is the messy version of Twister," Nikki explained. "Every time you land on a circle you have to put your hands or feet into the colored Jell-O."

"Oh, gross," I said.

"It gets real messy," said Nikki, "but it's guaranteed to make you laugh."

I got up from my lounge chair and we began to play. Soon we were covered with gooey Jell-O. But Nikki had been right. I was laughing.

Chapter Eleven

The next morning I woke up with the sun streaming in my face. I'd stayed up late the night before, working on my lines after everyone else went to sleep. I just hoped I remembered them today.

Chloe slept in the bed next to mine, her hand dangling over the side. "Chloe," I said. "Wake up. Today's your big day."

Her dark lashes fluttered open. "What?"

" 'Freshman Bell,' " I reminded her. "Isn't this the day you film your scenes?"

Chloe sat straight up. "That's right. What time is it?"

The digital clock read 7:30. "I'm supposed to be there at eight-thirty," Chloe said, leaping out of bed. She pulled her suitcase out from under the bed and flipped it open. "I suppose it doesn't matter what I wear. They said they'd have outfits for me."

"Are you nervous?" I asked.

"Not really," she said, pulling black-and-white-checked leggings from her case. "I just hope it will be fun."

She dressed quickly and ran a comb through her short hair. "Do you have the number of a cab company?" she asked me.

"You can get a ride with Cam," I told her. "I'll come with you."

"Should we let Nikki and Tracey sleep?" she asked.

"I guess so. They don't have to be on the set of *A Bridge of Love* until after lunch." I dressed in a white romper and stepped into sandals. "Ready," I said.

We went into the hall and met Tracey and Nikki, all dressed and ready to go. "We were going to let you sleep," I explained.

"And miss Chloe's TV debut? No way," said Nikki.

We had a quick breakfast of bagels and juice. Then Cam drove us to the studio, where the guard had Chloe's name on a list.

As soon as we stepped into the studio, the red-haired director Chloe and I had met on the beach rushed across the soundstage to greet Chloe. His name was Ty Mason. He was very nice to us, letting us sit and watch off to the side of the set, while Chloe was whisked away by the wardrobe person.

When Chloe came out of the wardrobe department, she was wearing a hot pink midriff top and flowered leggings. The hairstylist had spiked up her hair with gel. She looked great.

For her first bit, Chloe had to trip over some suitcases on a hotel landing and stumble down three steps right into the regular "Freshman Bell" cast.

She did the fall perfectly, then rolled to her feet and kept walking as if nothing had happened. Nikki, Tracey, and I burst out laughing. Chloe was turning out to be a natural comedian.

"It's a take!" shouted Ty through his laughter. "Perfect."

For her next scene, Chloe changed into another colorful outfit. This time she headed past one of the characters who was playing a busboy. She walked right in his path, causing him to drop a tray of dishes, which smashed to the floor all around him. Again, Chloe's character just kept walking.

After two more similar scenes, the geeky character who was supposed to have fallen in love with Chloe's character watched as she stepped into an elevator. As the doors slammed in his face, he sighed, "My mystery woman. How will I ever find her now?"

"Just follow the sound of breaking glass," said the

best-friend character.

That was all Chloe had to do. "You were great, better than great," Ty told her. "How would you feel about appearing in some more episodes?"

"It would be fun," said Chloe, "but I won't be in Hollywood for more than another week."

"Another week," Ty said thoughtfully. "Maybe we can work something up fast. Or maybe we can shoot an episode on location closer to you. Let me get back to you."

"Sure," Chloe said with a smile.

"You were wonderful," Nikki told her.

"Thanks," said Chloe. "What time is it?"

I checked my watch and saw that it was nearly twelve. "I'll call Cam," I said. I went down the hall to where I remembered seeing a pay phone. Before I could get there, something else caught my eye. It was a folded newspaper tossed on a metal chair. Even from a distance, I could see that the front page featured a picture of someone climbing out of a pool. It wasn't hard to guess who that someone was.

With a quick breath, I snatched up the paper. It was the *Daily Grapevine,* a cheap paper that was really just a gossip sheet. TAYLOR ANDREWS' KIDS RUN WILD AT POSH HOTEL blared the headline.

There I was, looking fuming mad as my hat leaked all over me. Another picture showed Johnny with his fists up as he yelled at Wilcox in the hotel dining room. We looked like two raving lunatics.

Quickly I turned to the inside page and read the story. It sounded as if Johnny and I had burst into the hotel and tried to terrorize everyone and make a mess. There wasn't anything true in the whole article! I couldn't believe it.

Chloe, Nikki, and Tracey came up behind me. "Did you call?" Tracey asked.

"Not yet."

They looked over my shoulder at the paper. "Not exactly the most flattering picture I've seen of you," Tracey commented dryly. "I've seen your brother look better, too."

"That's putting it mildly," I replied glumly. "How can I go to the studio now? How can I face everybody? Delia will love this. I bet she'll make sure everyone sees it."

"You have to go," Chloe said. "What other choice do you have?"

"None, I suppose," I said with a sigh. "Let me call Cam."

I did, and Cam said he would be over in less than ten minutes. But instead of Cam, Dad pulled up in his sports car.

"Hi," I said as I walked to the car with Chloe, Nikki, and Tracey behind me. "I thought you were at the studio."

"Not today," he explained. "Cam told me you called, but I said I'd get you."

I looked at him a moment, then realized why he was there. "You saw the *Daily Grapevine,* didn't you?"

"Yeah," he said, nodding. "Come on, get in."

"Are you upset?" I asked as I got into the front seat beside him.

"Yes," he said seriously. "I'm upset that it doesn't say 'Ted Hoffritz's Kids Run Wild.' What am I—a nobody around here?"

"Dad!" I laughed.

"No, I'm not upset, and neither is your mother," he said.

"You talked to her?" I asked.

"Yes, she's fine. She's only worried about you and Johnny. In the course of her career, she's had more crazy stories written about her than you would believe. She knows how it is."

"See?" said Nikki from the backseat. "It will be okay."

"Sure it will," said Dad, ruffling the top of my hair.

I smiled at him. I was angry that he'd been so busy during my visit, but it was good to know he was there for me when it counted.

When I walked into the studio, I was pretty nervous. Larry was right there, almost as if he'd been waiting by the door for me. "Got your lines down?" he asked me.

"Yes," I said.

"Good," he said. "I know you've been very busy running wild and all."

I groaned and shook my head dismally. "You saw the paper."

"It wasn't her fault," Tracey began. "I was there, and believe me, if anyone's to blame, it's—"

Larry held up his hand to stop her. "Relax, it was great," he said.

"What?" Chloe gasped, obviously as shocked as I was.

"Sure. The story inside talks about how you've been feuding with Delia. Apparently the *Grapevine* reporter had already gotten wind of that story. He wrote all about the movie we're shooting. And now the whole world knows you're Taylor Andrews' daughter and Johnny Renee's sister. They'll tune in to see you on TV for that reason alone. The studio couldn't have gotten this much publicity if they'd spent thousands of dollars. The producers are thrilled."

"Great, I guess," I said.

"Definitely great," he agreed. He looked at Chloe, Nikki, and Tracey. "What you're wearing is fine for now. I want to shoot some general hallway, changing classes scenes. Go over to set three. Ashley, go see Emily in wardrobe and then tell Kara in makeup I want a no-makeup look for you. Don't even bother going to hair—just wear it plain."

"All right," I said. As I went down the hall toward the makeup room, it seemed to me that the cast and crew members were smiling and nodding at me more than before. One of the extras gave me a thumbs-up, and another made an okay circle with his fingers.

"Well, you don't look any the worse for wear," joked Emily, the plump, gray-haired woman in charge of wardrobe.

"No, I just got wet," I told her, smiling for the first time since I'd seen the paper.

She found a plain T-shirt, a pair of baggy jeans, and a cardigan for me to wear. "This isn't exactly the kind of clothing you're used to wearing as a model," she commented.

"It's fine," I said. "It fits my character."

"You're right," Emily agreed. "Okay, go see Kara. She's the tall woman across the hall."

I went into the makeup room and spotted a very tall woman with dark hair. "It's the pool queen!" she joked when she saw me. "Have a seat."

"Larry says he wants a no-makeup look," I told her.

"Okay, that means lots of makeup in neutral tones. You're so pretty you hardly need it, but those close-ups can kill you if you're not wearing any."

"It's the same in modeling," I said.

When she was done, I brushed my hair and let it hang loose. Then I headed back down the hall toward the set. On the way, I saw Jack. "Hi," he said. "Congratulations on making the front page. In this town, that's tough to do."

"It's pretty embarrassing," I said. "Still, everyone has been so nice about it."

"That's because they all like you better," he said.

"What do you mean?"

"Before this happened, you were just a beautiful blond model who was related to famous people. Now you're more like a real person."

"I always was a real person," I objected.

"But now everyone knows it," he pointed out.

That seemed so silly that it really made me smile. "Thanks for yesterday," I told him. "You were so nice."

"No sweat," he said. "It was good to get to know you better." We continued walking together. When we got to the set, crowds of kids were pretending to walk through a junior high hallway.

Soon it was time to work on my scenes—and time to see Delia once again. She came onto the set and looked at me smugly. "Oh, if it isn't the little mermaid!" she said with a smirk.

I glared at her. "Buzz off, Delia."

"Ohhh," she breathed. "Someone is in a bad mood today."

"Let's take it from act three," Larry said. Delia groaned loudly. "Is something the matter, Delia?" Larry asked.

"Working with *her* is the matter," Delia said for all to hear. "She can't act. She can't even remember her lines.

Face it, casting her was a mistake."

That was it! She'd gone too far. "Delia, I'm sick of you. If you want to see what I can do, just watch." I whirled around toward Larry. "If I don't have this scene down and it isn't good, fire me."

"Ashley, I'm not going to—" he began.

"You heard her," Delia cut him off. "I think it's only fair." She turned toward the other actors. "After this scene, give a thumbs-up if it's any good, or thumbs-down if you think she should give up."

"That's enough," Larry told Delia. "I don't want to see any thumbs," he told the others. "This is not a contest."

But now it was. I knew that despite Larry's words, everyone would be watching and judging me.

Still, I was strangely confident. This time I had an image in my head. I thought of Samantha, Jack's sister. Even though she was older than my character, she was in the same dilemma. She wanted to fit in at a school where the kids were all much wealthier, but she didn't want to change herself or be anybody other than who she really was. I said my lines as if I was Samantha, and it really seemed to work. At least Larry never stopped me.

I could tell from Delia's scowling face that I was doing well. She wasn't pleased I was winning.

The final proof that I'd found my way into Julie's character came after I told Andrea, Delia's character, that I didn't need her pity. When I was done, I stood there, nearly breathless with the emotion of the scene. There was silence.

Without a word, Delia walked off the set.

And then I heard applause.

The cast and crew were applauding for me!

Chapter Twelve

———◆———

I hope I don't catch anything,"
I told Jack several days later as we stood on a bridge with
fishing poles dangling toward the water below.

"Why not?" he asked.

"Because I would feel so sorry for the fish," I explained.
"I'd just want to let it go."

Jack laughed and shook his head. "Then why did you
agree to come fishing with me?"

"It sounded like a nice way to spend the morning," I said.
"Before I thought about the fish, that is. Besides, we have
only another week of filming. I wanted to spend some time
together before I go home."

In the process of working on the movie, Jack and I had become good friends. I'd never had a guy friend before, but I found it wasn't all that different from having girlfriends. Except that I'd have felt funny talking about clothes and hair and stuff. Otherwise, it was pretty much the same.

"I'll miss you," he said, looking down at the water.

"I'll be back in the spring," I told him. "That's when I usually visit my dad. Chloe might come with me. The people at 'Freshman Bell' want her to shoot another couple of episodes."

"What about you?" he asked. "Do you think you'll be doing more TV or movies?"

"I don't think so," I said. "Being a model is what I really love. Doing this movie has taught me that."

"I'm surprised to hear you say that," he said. "Being an actress meant so much to you when you first got here."

I jiggled my line in the water, sending ripples out into the bay. "It seems like a lot of things have changed in me in a short time," I said.

"What kinds of things?" Jack asked.

"It's sort of hard to explain," I said. I leaned over the bridge and saw my reflection, all shimmery in the water. "See that person down there in the water? When I look at her, I see somebody special now. Not Ashley the model or Ashley the actress, but just Ashley, herself." I looked up at him. "And you know what? You helped me see myself—you, my brother, and my friends. You're the people who could really see me."

We fished for another hour. Jack caught two fish. And, just as I'd expected, I felt very sorry for them. Luckily, I caught nothing.

After a while, I looked at my watch and saw that it was nearly eleven-thirty. "I'd better be getting back," I told Jack. "My mother is flying home today, and I promised to have lunch with her."

Jack began reeling in his line. "We both have to be at the studio by two, anyway. You and I have to do our last scene together."

He and I had a scene where he tells me not to care about the other kids. At the end, we hug and promise always to be there for each another. It was a nice, warm scene, and I was glad that Jack was the one playing my brother. In a few days, we'd film some more scenes and be done. Larry had arranged for all the kids' scenes to be shot first, so everyone who needed to could return to school. He'd spend another two weeks filming scenes with the adults.

We got on our bikes and rode away from the bridge. Jack was slowed down by the bucket of fish hanging from his handlebars. I waved and turned off toward the Azure Shores Hotel, where I'd be meeting my mother.

As soon as I arrived, I went straight to the ladies'

room and changed into a blue sundress patterned with sunflowers. It was from the modeling shoot. I'd bought it with some of the money I'd earned.

Mom was already in the dining room when I got there. She looked elegant as always in a navy blue blazer and white slacks. "Ashley, sweetheart, hi," she said as I came to the table.

"Hi, Mom," I said. "You'll never guess what I did this morning. I went fishing!"

Mom wrinkled her nose. "I'm afraid that was never my favorite pastime. Did you catch anything?"

"No."

"Oh, thank heavens," she said. That made me smile. In a lot of ways, my mother and I are very much alike.

When the waiter came, Mom ordered red snapper. I ordered a salad. After staring those fish in the eye, I didn't know if I'd ever be able to eat fish again.

"Larry Morton let me see some of the unedited film," Mom told me when the waiter left. "You look like an angel. Your acting is terrific, too. You really come off well."

"Thanks," I said. I was really pleased. No matter what the future held, I wanted to do well in this movie. My mother's opinion counted. She was a professional, and she was, well . . . my mother.

She put a small, wrapped box on the table and slid it toward me. "This is for you," she said.

I smiled and took it. "What for?"

"For nothing. Open it," she said.

I unwrapped the box and opened the lid. Inside was a silver necklace with a silver heart. "It's beautiful," I said sincerely as I put it on.

"I was in the jeweler's looking for something to get you," she said. "You know, something to remind you of me since we'll be apart for a while longer. And I saw a necklace with a charm of a racehorse. I thought to myself, that's perfect for Ashley. She's a champion, and I want her to know I think so."

"But you decided against it," I said, wondering why.

"I was just about to pay for it when I changed my mind," she went on. "I asked the salesclerk for the heart instead. I decided it was more important that you remember how much I love you."

"Even if I'm never a famous actress?" I dared to ask.

"No matter what," she said.

I leaned across the table and hugged my mother, burying my head against her shoulder. In all the world, she couldn't have found a better gift or any words I'd rather have heard.

We finished lunch, and then Johnny joined us for dessert. He was going to drive Mom to the airport. "You won't believe this," he said as he took his seat. "The writers on the show are working on a story where my character is fixing the telephone of a famous actress. He gets into a fight with a photographer and lands in jail. The actress comes and bails him out, and they have a big romance. The writers say they want to make the most of the publicity I got from my fight with Wilcox."

Mom laughed as she stirred her coffee. "That's the weird world of TV for you. But, listen, I don't want to read more stories about my kids running wild."

"I promise," said Johnny.

"Well, I can't promise I won't slip into a pool again." I laughed. "But Delia has been leaving me alone, so I don't think there will be any problems."

"Good," said Mom, smiling at us both.

Our words were put to the test on the way out. Mr. Wilcox appeared in the lobby, almost as if he'd come out of nowhere. Of course he walked right up to us, shooting pictures a mile a minute.

"That guy . . ." Johnny grumbled.

"Remember your promise," Mom reminded him. "I know how we can *really* ruin his day." She stepped aside so that Johnny was on one side of her and I was on the other. She put her arms around us and whispered, "Smile and wave."

That's what we did. We waved at Wilcox like he was our best friend in the world.

Instantly, he stopped taking pictures. His face turned red with anger, and he stomped off.

"He knows he'll never be able to sell a picture of a

happy, smiling family." Mom laughed. "Nobody cares about that story."

I smiled, proud of my mother. I cared about that story. And I was very glad to be part of it.

Chapter Thirteen

———◆———

I flicked the light switch on the wall, and the photographer's darkroom was instantly awash in red light. It was good to be home. After two weeks in California, we were finally back in our secret place, the Red Room, at the Calico Modeling Agency.

Nikki, Chloe, and Tracey scurried into the room behind me. "Are you guys ready for this?" Chloe giggled as she fished around in her black-and-white-checked vinyl tote bag.

"Come on, quit the suspense," Tracey urged as she boosted herself onto the narrow table against the wall. "Let's see it!"

With a twinkle in her eye, Chloe pulled out the brand-new issue of *TV Today*. The pocket-sized magazine was full of listings and carried stories about TV stars, too. Guess who was on the cover? Chloe, Nikki, Tracey, and me! CALICO JUNIOR MODELS GO HOLLYWOOD! was the headline.

The story had been Kate Calico's idea. She'd contacted the magazine and set up the interviews and all. We'd never dreamed they would put our pictures on the front cover.

Of course my face has been on the cover of lots of magazines. But the story inside was never about me or my friends before!

"Delia Carrol must be going crazy with jealousy," Nikki laughed.

"It serves her right after all the trouble she gave Ashley," added Tracey.

"Look at this," said Chloe, thumbing through the magazine. She folded the pages back and showed us a black-and-white photo of herself falling down the stairs on the set of "Freshman Bell." " 'Chloe Chang shows an unexpected flair for comedy,' " she said, reading the caption under the photo. Her first "Freshman Bell" appearance would be shown on television this week, along with my movie, *A Bridge of Love.*

"Since winning the modeling contest, so many exciting things have happened to me," said Nikki with a dreamy look in her eyes. "But so far, I'd say that going to Hollywood has been the most exciting."

Tracey cocked her head thoughtfully. "I don't know," she said. "Being chosen as the Dingaling Cupcake girl was pretty thrilling."

Nikki pushed her playfully. We all knew Tracey hated being the Dingaling Cupcake girl. She thought it was dumb, and didn't even like all their cupcakes. "Okay." Tracey laughed. "Maybe being in a TV movie was just *slightly* more exciting."

"Just slightly," Nikki said with laughter in her voice. "Six months ago, I'd never have dreamed I'd be seeing myself on TV, even if I am only sitting in a classroom and walking down a crowded hall. My friends from school have arranged to have a party at my friend Dee's house that night so they can all watch me walk down the hall together."

"My parents are having two TVs placed in their restaurant the night 'Freshman Bell' is on," said Chloe. "They're serving free appetizers to anyone who comes in while the show is on—which will be just about everyone in my neighborhood."

"My mother and her boyfriend are taking me out to dinner after the movie airs," Tracey admitted sheepishly.

At my house, it would be much less of a big deal. After all, I didn't bother to watch Mom's show every morning anymore. I didn't even always watch "One

Ashford Avenue." But Mom had promised to stay home that night so we could watch *A Bridge of Love* together. "We'll order pizza in," she'd said. That was the best thing she could have suggested. If she'd thrown a big party with a zillion people and scattered a hundred TV sets around the room, I wouldn't have felt nearly as good.

It was funny, but on the outside, I'm sure I still looked and sounded like the same old Ashley. But, inside, something was different—better, stronger. I'd learned some things about myself and about my friends, too. "You guys would be my friends even if I was just a regular girl with no career, wouldn't you?" I said. It wasn't really a question. I knew they would be.

"Of course," said Chloe.

"We may not be models forever," said Nikki. "But I hope we'll be friends forever."

"Me, too," added Tracey quietly.

"We will be," I said, smiling confidently. "Friends forever!"